THE ALIENS STEP IN

DEFENDERS OF TIME | BOOK 3

THE ALIENS STEP IN

BEST SELLING AUTHOR

GENE P. ABEL

The Aliens Step In
© 2023 by Gene P. Abel

This is a work of fiction. Names, characters, places, and incidents either are the product of the author's imagination or are used fictitiously. Any resemblance to actual events, locales, or persons, living or dead, is entirely coincidental.

All rights reserved. No portion of this publication may be reproduced, stored in a retrieval system, or transmitted by any means—electronic, mechanical, photocopying, recording, or any other—except for brief quotations in printed reviews, without the prior written permission of the publisher.

Editors: River Chau, Deborah Froese, Debra Wallace
Illustrator: Gus Duemas (Illustration on page 93 by Joshua Smith.)
Cover Design: Presslytica U.S.
Interior Design: Emma Elzinga

Indigo River Publishing
3 West Garden Street, Ste. 718
Pensacola, FL 32502
www.indigoriverpublishing.com

Ordering Information:
Quantity Sales: Special discounts are available on quantity purchases by corporations, associations, and others. For details, contact the publisher at the address above.
Orders by US trade bookstores and wholesalers: Please contact the publisher at the address above.

Printed in the United States of America

Library of Congress Control Number: 2023938480
ISBN: 978-1-954676-55-8 (paperback)   978-1-954676-56-5 (ebook)

First Edition

With Indigo River Publishing, you can always expect great books, strong voices, and meaningful messages. Most importantly, you'll always find . . . *words worth reading.*

CONTENTS

1	Wedding Day	1
2	Black Ops Blues	9
3	Stealing The Future	20
4	Taking Charge	29
5	The New Mission	34
6	Getting Started	41
7	The First Chase	46
8	Question Time	50
9	The Chinese Device	54
10	Getting In	60
11	Double Chase	67
12	The Intervention	76
13	Unexpected Visitor	83
14	Tour Of Force	89
15	Return	104
16	Debriefing	107
17	Personal Feelings	113
18	Assembling	116
19	Trip to An Alien World	121
20	Arrival	133
21	Interrogation	142
22	Waiting Room	149
23	Alien Chase	159
24	Bomb!	169
25	Audience	181
26	Exchange	198
27	Agent Hessman's Decision	212
	Illustrations	215

"To my beautiful and totally supportive wife, Susan Anne who is always there to encourage and support all that I do."

Gene

CHAPTER ONE
WEDDING DAY

THE BRIDE WAS DRESSED IN WHITE, and her train flowed like a ripple of sea foam behind her as she walked up the aisle with her fatherly escort. The groom waited nervously by the altar with his best man beside him. The pair stood across from the maid of honor, who smiled as the bride performed her slow, stately walk toward the awaiting priest.

The bride, of course, was Claire Hill, a twentieth-century reporter transported to twenty-first century time. Her escort was Special Agent Lou Hessman. The nervous-looking groom, Professor Ben Stein, watched the girl of his dreams commence her slow approach in time to organ music. Dr. Sam Weiss stood on Ben's right as his best man, with Captain Robert Beck, a large muscular man, on Sam's right as another groomsman. The maid of honor, Agent Sue Harris, did more than simply smile for her friend; she kept an eye on the wedding crowd as well.

As for the priest, that would be General Karlson.

They weren't exactly in a church, however. More like a small convention hall in Los Alamos, with organ music piped over the hall's speakers. The crowd filling the makeshift pews was composed of various personnel

THE ALIENS STEP IN

from the secret base where they worked together, people who had come to know Miss Hill over the recent months. The hall had been decorated to resemble a church, though one with a Hawaiian theme, complete with projections on the walls of Hawaiian beaches and palm trees swaying in the breeze.

As Claire approached the altar on Agent Hessman's arm, she saw Sue whisper into the tiny mic Claire had helped her hide within the collar of her long blue gown. Claire strained her ears to listen.

"I see someone making a break for it in the back. Check him out . . . bathroom break? Well tell Simmons that he can go later and get him back in his seat," Sue hissed. "We're here for Claire . . . How's the north perimeter . . . I don't care *whose* kid that is, no touching the buffet until the bride and groom do . . . Keep an eye out for anything—snipers, rogue Russian time travelers, someone's pet cat—for all we know, some future time has turned house cats into spies . . . Carl, nudge Ted awake and tighten up that perimeter. This wedding is going off without a hitch if I have to carry the bride and groom across the threshold myself."

Claire smiled. Counting the fourteen armed soldiers hidden around the outside of the convention hall, this was probably the most secure wedding Los Alamos had seen in a long time. As she halted before her groom, the music faded away. Agent Hessman gave her a quick kiss on the cheek, and she hugged him in return.

Agent Hessman took his seat in the front row as the ceremony got underway.

General Karlson smiled at Claire and Ben and then addressed the hall. "Ladies and Gentlemen, I have been granted an authority usually reserved for priests and captains at sea, but because of our highly unusual circumstances, I have the privilege to preside over this most happy of occasions. Two of our own from . . . well, let's just say that they'll have a rather interesting story to tell their children about how they met."

A few chuckles circulated the large room.

"We have before us Professor Ben Stein, a man who had to go farther out of his way than anyone else I've heard of to find the love of his life," the general continued. "He's an unassuming man of letters and compassion whose head can be said to be lost in the past. For his bride, we have Claire Hill, late of another century. She has become an invaluable member of our team and a dear friend, somewhere between being everyone's younger sister and our mascot. All things considered, I can think of no one more appropriate to be Ben's bride."

A small murmur of agreement arose. Claire smiled at Ben and felt the warmth of his loving gaze through her veil.

The general cleared his throat, and the murmuring faded. "The couple decided to write their own vows," he said.

We certainly did, Claire thought. *And then we had to run each word past Security Chief Hessman.*

"Ben," General Karlson continued, "let's begin with you."

Ben took a slip of paper out of his tuxedo pocket and began speaking—with a slight stutter. Then his eyes locked onto Claire's. She held his gaze, and it felt as though only the two of them existed.

"I've always had a love of the past, of history, but never in my life did I suspect that I would have a chance to literally fall in love with something from that past, to hold it tight in my arms. Claire Hill, you of the past have become my future, my reason for continuing. As a historian, I once vowed to cherish the past. Now, as a groom, I vow to love and protect you as its representative, to hold you close, protect you from all the unusual dangers that seem to beset us. You are the light of my soul, and there is nothing that I will not do to keep that light smiling brightly."

Ben looked at the general and nodded. The general turned to Claire, and she moistened her lips.

"Ben," she began, "every girl imagines a shining knight to come rescue her, but I never thought that mine would come from, well, so far away. You literally rescued me, saved my life, and captured my heart. I'd always thought I was born for a different time. I guess that was truer than I could have imagined. Ben Stein, I promise to stand by your side, to face together whatever there may be, whenever it may be. You are my knight, and I am your warrior maiden with a quill. I will never leave your side."

She smiled at Ben, and the two turned to General Karlson.

"Moving speeches for both," the general acknowledged. "There remains one last thing to do. I believe someone has a ring?"

Claire raised her eyebrows, encouraging Ben to respond to the general, but Ben was too fixated on her eyes to see anything else.

Dr. Weiss winked at Claire and, with his cane, nudged Ben from behind. Ben jumped and turned to face Dr. Weiss, who extended his right hand, a gold ring glittering in his palm.

"My boy," Dr. Weiss whispered with a grin, "I know you want to skip straight to the honeymoon, but you've got to put this ring on her first."

"Thanks, my friend," Ben whispered back, taking the ring.

Ben turned to face Claire, who was trembling. Sue placed a steadying hand on her shoulder as Ben took Claire's left hand in his.

"Claire," he said quietly, "my soul is yours." He slid the ring onto her finger.

"And mine is yours," Claire replied in the same quiet tone.

Sue slipped a wedding band into Claire's palm, and Claire slid it over Ben's finger, locking eyes with him.

The general cleared his throat again. "If anyone present objects to this union . . . well, they can just take it up with Sue."

The Maid of Honor set her face into a snarl and regarded the audience in challenge.

No one spoke, but there were a few smiles.

"In that case," the general continued, "by the authority invested in me by various government agencies so secret that merely mentioning their names would get me into trouble, I now pronounce you husband and wife. You may kiss the bride."

Ben raised Claire's veil, and the newlyweds exchanged loving looks before bringing their lips together. Their kiss turned into an embrace punctuated by the sudden explosion of recorded wedding music.

The general boldly announced, "Ladies and gentlemen, I now present Mr. and Mrs. Stein!"

As Claire and her new husband turned to face their guests, the crowd rose to its feet in applause.

Claire felt Sue's hand on her shoulder again, and she turned.

"See you shortly," Sue said, abruptly tucking her chin toward her mic. "Yes . . . uh huh . . ." she whispered. "No way. He doesn't get to do that . . ."

Claire turned back to Ben. Clutching arms, the couple from out of time marched down the aisle together, their lives as one begun.

☾

The wedding reception took place in an adjoining convention hall, the décor continuing the Hawaiian theme. The smell of pulled pork and pineapple roasting on the grill made everyone think they had been transported to Hawaii. A government-approved service, cleared by both Lou and Sue, catered the food.

The wedding cake, a marvel of culinary engineering, depicted the city of New York as it looked in 1919 and today. Half of it was decorated with a horse-drawn carriage, while the other side had modern New York Skyscrapers. While Ben and Claire cut the first slice together, Sue took pictures.

General Karlson offered his personal congratulations and strode to the main table where Agent Hessman sat next to Dr. Weiss. The pair were speaking quietly.

"Just some fascinating developments I've been reading about of late," Dr. Weiss was saying.

The general sat next to Dr. Weiss, who turned from Agent Hessman to face the general. "You heard, of course, about the Kamioka facility in Japan picking up its first gravity waves a couple years back," he continued excitedly. "Well, now they've linked up with the Ligo and Virgo facilities to effectively create a globe-spanning gravity wave detector. Why, the possibilities—"

"Sam," the general interrupted, "while I'm sure that's quite interesting, it's a little bit outside my field."

"Oh, I'm sorry. As you know, I can get quite excited about certain things. But speaking of Ligo, they detected macroscopic movements on an eight-pound mirror that resulted from quantum fluctuations. Exceedingly minute, mind you, but worth keeping an eye on since that level of accuracy could prove useful in our own endeavors."

Agent Hessman nodded and reached for his water glass.

"Now that is something I'd be interested in hearing more about—uh, the layman's version of course," General Karlson said. "Anything that might improve the accuracy of our equipment. But later, after the reception."

"Oh, of course," Dr. Weiss said.

The general glanced at the bridal couple. Sue scooted around them, using her cell phone to take pictures from different angles.

"In relation to the great plastic disintegration incident that our future Russian friends suffered through, I recently read about scientists engineering an enzyme that digests plastic waste six times faster than would happen naturally."

The general raised an eyebrow and leaned toward Dr. Weiss.

Agent Hessman leaned forward too and spoke in a hushed tone. "Are you saying we're still going to have to go through another disaster like the one caused by the plastic-eating bug we developed to clean the oceans? The one that got loose in Russia and resulted in those Russians from the future coming back and causing us all that grief?"

"Not necessarily," Dr. Weiss noted. "In that particular future, a bug performed the task. It was able to escape and breed out in the open environment. Now, they're investigating the use of an enzyme rather than a bacterium that can escape and breed. The one event still happens but without the disastrous side-effect we experienced. I'll keep an eye on it, of course, but it seems because of the way things turned out . . . with my niece . . . we may have avoided that particular future."

Dr. Weiss looked distant for a moment. General Karlson didn't need to ask why. The doctor's niece still lay in a coma because of that same incident.

Dr. Weiss glanced toward the happy couple, who were now stuffing cake into each others' mouths. His frown dissolved into a smile. He turned back to General Karlson and Agent Hessman. "So, if we do something that creates problems across time, we'll know how long we have to fix it. The temporal neutral field has been tested and seems to be good for twenty-four hours."

"The only thing going wrong right now is that new observer in from China," Agent Hessman replied.

"Oh, that's right. China is interested in developing their own time travel program. For historical purposes," Dr. Weiss replied. "They want to examine certain portions of their own ancient history."

"That's the cover story we're supposed to buy," Agent Hessman said. "I'm not taking my eyes off Doctor Howard Ping for a second."

General Karlson glanced at the bridal couple again. They stood by a table full of sliced cake. Time for the first dance. As if on cue, music began. The general rose and approached the bride. He escorted her onto the floor for a "father" and daughter dance. Sue followed shortly with Ben.

☾

Agent Hessman remained at the table studying the newlyweds. He wished them a happy and uneventful life, but he knew better than to expect it.

The music changed, and the general released Claire. Captain Beck began to dance with her.

Agent Hessman's phone buzzed in his pocket. He took it out and glanced at the display. He frowned and raised his hand, nodding at the general.

General Karlson approached with a pleasant smile on his face, but as he sat next to Agent Hessman, the quiet tone of his voice betrayed concern. "I don't care if the world just ended, we're not ruining their day, Hessman. So nice and quiet, tell me; what's the problem?"

"That new black ops team just arrived. They're taking possession of Chamber Two," Agent Hessman reported.

"They're early," the general replied in an annoyed whisper.

"Black ops?" Dr. Weiss broke in. "What's a black ops team doing in a time travel facility?"

"Your guess is as good as mine," the general replied. "It's one of the concessions I had to make to keep things going and get the second chamber installed. They get some limited use of the secondary chamber, and we still have a budget." He sighed. "Okay, keep an eye on it but nothing to make the happy couple suspicious. With Miss Hill's—Mrs. Hill-*Stein's*—reporter instincts, she might catch onto nearly anything."

Agent Hessman nodded as Claire approached. "Lou, I've reserved the next dance for you," she beamed, extending her hand. "Now, come on."

Agent Hessman found himself pulled out onto the dance floor by the new bride as a line of well-wishers swarmed around the groom, reaching to shake his hand and stuff a few bucks into his pouch to help the couple begin their new life together.

"Congratulations, Miss Hill," Agent Hessman said as they danced.

"First off, it's Mrs. Hill-Stein now; I'm keeping the 'Hill' in there for my byline. And second, it's *Claire*."

"As you wish, *Claire*," Agent Hessman said with a smile. "Normally I would ask where you're going on your honeymoon, but since I made the security arrangements . . . Have a great time in Hawaii."

"We will," she replied. "And thank you for everything. If you hadn't called Ben in as a consultant for that first time-travel mission, I'd have never met him. The chances are just beyond astronomical, and for that, you have my eternal thanks."

Their dance ended with a hug and a kiss from Claire, who then turned to Dr. Weiss. The two of them made quite a pair on the dance floor as the good doctor tried to manage his cane.

Shortly after that, Agent Hessman watched Ben and Claire Stein quietly disappear from the wedding reception for their honeymoon.

CHAPTER TWO
BLACK OPS BLUES

SLIGHTLY MORE THAN TWO WEEKS later, the newlyweds took an elevator down to the underground portion of the secret base. The door opened to face a drab wall stenciled with directions. *Headquarters* had an arrow pointing to the right, while *Personnel Quarters* pointed left.

Claire stepped off the elevator first. She wore a knee-length summer dress which seemed more appropriate for Hawaii than the middle of the New Mexico desert. Her pearly white skin sported a new tan that went well with her long tresses of black hair. She held onto Ben's arm. He was back to dressing in his usual baggy clothes.

Another person stepped off the elevator behind them—a dark-haired man who looked much like an accountant.

"You must be Miss Stein," the accountant said as the elevator doors closed. "I've been hearing about you."

"Thank you," Claire beamed, "but that's *Hill*-Stein now. At least that's how my future bylines will read."

"I'm Mr. Thomas."

He extended his hand, and she took it briefly.

"I don't recognize you. Are you new here?" Ben asked.

"I'm a government observer," Mr. Thomas replied. "I'm just here to make sure that mistakes don't happen."

As Ben and Claire turned to the left and began walking briskly toward personnel quarters, Sue burst through the stairwell.

"Sue!" Claire beamed, hugging the most feared operative in the base as though they were sisters.

The elevator door opened again, and Dr. Weiss and Agent Hessman exited. They marched quickly to catch up with the other three friends.

"Ben, my boy," Dr. Weiss said, clasping Ben's forearm.

"With your cane and that kind of greeting, people will think you're twenty years my senior," Ben chuckled. "I'm a year older than you."

"All part of the image I'm trying to conjure around this cane of mine." Dr. Weiss smiled. "I suppose a smoking jacket might be next in order. So, how was the honeymoon? Did you take in Heavenly Hana like I suggested?"

"Yes, and it *was* heavenly," Claire said. "The road trip to Hana was very exciting! I will never forget the feeling we were going to dive over the edge of the road."

Together, they continued along the thoroughfare and through a final security check with scanners. Their meandering walk continued with an equally meandering conversation.

". . . but according to the scuttlebutt," Dr. Weiss was saying, "the Pentagon is going to be making some of their UFO findings public."

"Probably to cover up for any news on time travel," Ben chuckled. "I've heard all the same rumors. Everything from the Pentagon having some off-world vehicles in their possession, to someone mathematically proving the reason we've never seen evidence of any aliens."

"Why's that?" Agent Hessman asked.

"Because they kill themselves off once they reach a certain level of development," Ben replied. "All hokum."

"This," Claire interjected with a smile, "from a man whose wife died a hundred years ago?"

Dead of influenza is what Claire would have been if Ben had left her back in the year 1919 when he'd found her during their first-time travel experience.

"Me thinks the lady won the argument," Dr. Weiss remarked with a grin.

"At least if I know what's good for me," Ben replied with a smile of his own. He took Claire's arm and gave it a loving squeeze.

"You know, I have been hearing about a significant uptick in the number of UFO sightings lately," Dr. Weiss continued.

"Oh?" Claire slowed down to peer at him.

"Yes," Dr. Weiss replied. "And that includes one just the other day not a dozen or so miles away from here and rumors of sightings in China."

"Hmm," Claire mused. "I wonder if there's a story in there."

"Now look what you've done," Ben remarked. "You've gotten her started."

"Again," Dr. Weiss grinned. "Sorry."

"In fact," Claire continued, "maybe those UFOs are actually alien spaceships. I've never interviewed an alien before and—"

"Aliens?" Ben interjected. "Really?"

Dr. Weiss shrugged. "Well, some of those UFO blips *have* been making what might be termed as course corrections. Just saying."

A foreboding Black man, followed by a line of well-built men in dark-colored body armor, headed toward the group of five. They looked ominous with menacing weapons and helmets that had built-in com-links. With barely a sour glance, the leader bumped into Claire as he and his men rudely pushed through the group.

"Hey, watch where you're going," Ben objected with a protective arm around Claire. "You bumped into my wife."

"This is no place for civilians," the leader growled.

"I know there's been some upgraded base security," Claire remarked as she watched them pass. "But do they have to be so rude?"

"They're not my people," Agent Hessman explained tersely. "That's

Colonel Cassidy and his team. They're here for purposes of their own, none of which I'm officially privy to."

"And unofficially?" Ben prompted.

They turned down a branching corridor labelled *Personnel Quarters*, walking past some other residents who were coming and going. All of them were far more polite than the colonel's team had been, greeting Claire with a nod and a smile.

"The colonel and his men are black ops," Agent Hessman explained. "They've permanently commandeered Chamber Two for their own purposes. Their missions are usually brief, but whenever they go out, they have their own people at the controls and actually black out the temporal detection grid so they can't be tracked."

"But that's insane!" Ben said. "How do you know what they're doing? What if something goes wrong?"

"Among the many concerns we all share," Dr. Weiss observed. "The general especially worries about them since this place, and pretty much history itself now, is his responsibility."

"Then why let them in?" Claire asked. "Give them the boot."

"Love to," Agent Hessman said as he brought them to a halt in front of a larger set of living quarters. "Unfortunately, their presence is beyond our control. It's the price we're paying to keep this place running. All we know about their missions is that whenever they leave the temporal chamber, they carry metal lock boxes that they didn't have when they arrived. As base security chief, I've asked about them, of course, but Colonel Cassidy says that it's— and I'm quoting here— 'above my pay grade.'"

"I'd like to take that colonel's paygrade," Sue began, "and shove it up his—"

"How long has this been going on?" Ben interrupted.

"They came on base during the wedding reception a couple of weeks ago," Dr. Weiss replied. "We didn't want to interrupt your happy mood."

"For which we thank you, Dr. Weiss." Claire smiled at her husband. "Now, could someone tell me why we're standing in front of this door? My quarters are down the hall and around the corner."

"Not anymore," Dr. Weiss announced with a grin. "I reminded General Karlson that a couple needs a bigger room to bounce around in. So, we moved your belongings and Ben's into these new quarters."

"It's technically an officer's quarters," Agent Hessman told them. "That means two rooms and your own private bath. Sue here was in charge of moving your belongings, Claire."

"I wanted to personally make sure your things were arranged with care," Sue remarked. "That includes adding a special shelf for your budding collection of time-travel mementos."

"Oh, thank you—all of you," Claire beamed. "Ben, let's take a look." She led her husband into their new quarters.

"Take a little time to settle in. We'll meet you later," Agent Hessman said.

☾

Agent Hessman watched the door close behind the newlyweds before turning away—nearly bumping into a dark-haired man in the process.

"Who are you?" Agent Hessman demanded.

"Oh, I'm sorry. My name is Mr. Thomas. I'm the new government observer."

"Like we don't have enough problems with Colonel Cassidy's team." Sue rolled her eyes.

"Yeah, I do remember that memo crossing my desk, Mr. Thomas," Agent Hessman sighed. "You've been cleared through my security. Just make sure to stay out of the way."

"And don't touch anything," Dr. Weiss added. "There is some very delicate equipment around here."

"As I said, I am here only to observe." The man stepped away with a nod and disappeared into the shadows.

THE ALIENS STEP IN

☾

An hour later, Agent Hessman sat next to Samantha's bed studying her face and trying to ignore the equipment bleeping around her. Between the horrific implications of her situation and the faint but lingering scent of her gardenia perfume, his stomach knotted.

Someone knocked softly. He looked up to see Ben and Claire standing in the doorway.

"No change," he said.

"How often do you see her?" Ben asked.

"Not nearly as often as Dr. Weiss," Agent Hessman replied.

"This is heartbreaking," Claire reached for his shoulder. "How are you feeling?"

"What I feel does not matter." Agent Hessman replied crisply. "I... the nature of my profession permits no room in my life for such relationships."

"Utter balderdash," Claire snapped. "Here." She drew Agent Hessman in for a close hug, and he stiffened, uncomfortable with outward displays of emotion.

"If you won't cry, then I'll cry for the both of us." Claire's voice broke.

"Thank you, Claire." Agent Hessman's tone remained bland and unemotional, but inside, he wept.

As Sue released him, arguing voices approached.

"... As chief medical doctor of this facility, I cannot sanction the use of some new—"

"Sanction it anyway," replied a deep voice. "It's her only chance."

A doctor entered the room accompanied by the foreboding presence of Colonel Cassidy. Cassidy handed the doctor something that looked like a set of headphones. Agent Hessman immediately snapped back into his professional demeanor while Ben and Claire stepped aside, making room around the bed.

"What's going on? Colonel, are you trying to make trouble for the base medical personnel?" Agent Hessman asked.

"Not at all," came the gruff reply. "I'm actually trying to help." Colonel Cassidy held up the device as he explained. It looked like a set of high-tech headphones with a soft rubber pad on either side and wide band connecting them. A cylinder extending from the top of that band held a row of four buttons.

"This should revive your coma patient. The pads go on her forehead, and these buttons operate it. Press the first button to initiate the scan. When the light under it comes on, press the second button. If she doesn't show signs of improvement after an hour, then you can try the third button. Fourth button stops the treatment," Cassidy said.

"Miss Weiss is in a deep coma far beyond the reach of any technology that I am aware of," the doctor objected. "How do we know this toy will not make her even worse?"

"It's experimental," Colonel Cassidy stated. "However, I've seen it work myself. Use it if you want to get her back."

With no further pleas, he thrust the device into the doctor's hand and left. As the doctor slowly turned it over, Agent Hessman and Ben flanked his sides. Claire pulled up a chair and sat beside the sleeping Samantha.

"Is there any chance this thing can do what he says?" Agent Hessman asked.

"Not according to anything *I've* ever heard of. Her brain is a mess," the doctor replied. "I don't see how this little gadget could do anything."

"Could it make her any worse?" Ben asked.

"Not really," the doctor admitted. "I just don't see it doing anything at all."

"Then it should be Sam's decision as her uncle," Ben said.

"He has already given his approval," the doctor replied. "But he's very distraught and liable to approve anything with the remotest of chances. As a doctor, I can't simply—"

"Excuse me," Claire interjected. "Didn't the colonel say that he's seen it work? Samantha is worse than dead right now. I don't see what harm that would do if it had the slightest chance of working."

"You mean we should trust the colonel?" Agent Hessman asked.

"Trust? No. But he's not the type to outright lie. He's a soldier; if he doesn't want you to know something, he'll just tell you straight to your face that's the way it is. He said he has seen it work, so it must work."

"I'll admit," Agent Hessman said with a slight shrug, "that has been the colonel's way. He's never lied to me, just said that I don't have the clearance to know what he's up to. Doctor, if there is any chance that this technology can improve her condition, then I say do it. The alternative is to see Miss Weiss in that bed for . . . how long would you estimate?"

The doctor stared at his comatose patient and sighed. "Okay, I'll try it out. But don't get your hopes up. Miss Weiss's mind has been deeply fractured."

That said, the doctor walked over to the bed. Agent Hessman clenched his fists as the doctor placed the device around Samantha's head with pads on either side of her forehead. After a breath, he pressed the first button. For several seconds, it looked like nothing was happening. Just when the doctor was ready to take it off and be done with it, the light beneath that same button lit up.

"Well, according to what the colonel said, the scan is complete," the doctor stated. "But this gadget seems awfully small to provide a complete brain scan so quickly."

"Just give it a try," Claire pleaded. "Please?"

The doctor shrugged and pressed the second button. The light beneath it started blinking. Agent Hessman looked at his watch and wondered how long it would take to see the results.

"Maybe it just takes a while," Claire suggested.

"Or maybe it's another false hope," Agent Hessman decided. "I suggest we leave the doctor to be about—"

"I don't believe it!"

Agent Hessman's eyes moved to the doctor, who focused intently on one of the bedside monitors. It was one of the quieter machines, only now its silent rhythm had suddenly come alive with higher spikes than any he had seen in the past month.

Agent Hessman could not believe what he was seeing. "Doctor, does this mean what I think it does?"

"It's true," the doctor finally announced. "The strength of her EEG is up five percent and steadily climbing. With the other indicators . . . I just can't believe it."

"Doctor," Ben asked, "what are you saying?"

"He's talking about *that*." Claire pointed to Samantha, beaming.

Ben stared at Samantha's face until he saw what his keen-eyed reporter-wife had first noticed. "Her eyes are moving," he exclaimed.

Agent Hessman nodded. Not much movement, but it was there.

"REM sleep," the doctor said. "She's beginning to dream. Don't ask me how, but this thing is actually working."

"Miss Weiss is going to be okay?" Agent Hessman asked as a smile replaced his expression of concern.

The doctor rechecked a few of his monitors before daring to give a reply. "At this rate of improvement, it will be a few hours before she regains consciousness, but . . . yes, Miss Weiss should recover. Of course, there will have to be tests to determine the extent of any lingering brain damage, but my God! She's actually recovering!"

Claire jumped and clapped her fingers together while Ben nearly hugged the doctor instead of his wife.

Agent Hessman stepped over next to the bed, looking down at the intermittent flutter beneath Samantha's eyelids as the doctor rechecked his monitors. Without taking his gaze off Samantha, he said, "I'll have to offer the colonel my thanks. It appears his experimental technology is working."

"Experimental?" the doctor said as he looked up from his monitors and readings. "This does not look like experimental technology, and I cannot begin to explain it. I'm at a complete loss."

Agent Hessman cocked an eyebrow in the doctor's direction, and then his eyes narrowed. He rose to his feet and headed for the door.

THE ALIENS STEP IN

☾

Agent Hessman caught up with Colonel Cassidy in the hallway leading to Temporal Chamber Two. Mr. Thomas stood fifty feet away, typing a text on his cell phone as he watched the pair of them.

Agent Hessman approached Mr. Thomas. "That device is from the future," he said bluntly, his voice low. "Do you know how dangerous that makes what you're doing?"

The colonel was just as blunt in his reply—and just as quiet. "The way I see it, I'm simply balancing things out. People from the future interfered with our present by putting her in that condition, so I see no problem with using one of their toys to get her back. She's a very valuable commodity. Now, if you don't mind, I have a mission to be about." The colonel left at a brisk pace.

Dr. Weiss skipped around the corner wearing a big smile. "Did you hear? Sam's going to be all right! My niece will be okay. Oh, what miracles this day brings!"

Agent Hessman nodded. "I confronted the Colonel. He verified that the device he supplied came from the future. It's working, but it leaves me in a moral grey zone. He says he's just fixing what those future Russians did."

"Temporal causality can be a tricky thing," Dr. Weiss agreed. "If you look at things from a four-dimensional point of view—"

"Just the highlights, if you don't mind, Sam," said Agent Hessman. "Skip the ten-dollar words."

"Ah, well, what the colonel told you is essentially correct," Sam stated. "Some papers written on the subject say that time will heal itself. If you change one thing in the past, something else will happen to make up for it, thus eliminating the possibility of any real paradoxes. Well, *we* are the past from the perspective of those future Russians. They basically broke time a little, so it stands to reason that temporal causality would allow something from their time to come into our time to fix things up—in this case, my lovely niece."

"Allow? What do you mean?" Agent Hessman asked.

"Well, basically, many things from the future would either have no way to work back in our time. They'd be useless and out of place—like taking a cell phone back to the early twentieth century with no cellular networks. It wouldn't work. So, causality would allow whatever is required to fix the breakage those Russians created. Hence, we got the one device that works without needing any other futuristic support equipment."

"I see," Agent Hessman said. "But then, if the colonel were to bring back other things—"

A familiar air-raid alarm interrupted Agent Hessman, and a sign on the wall at the end of the hall flashed *Time Chamber in Use!*

Agent Hessman barely noticed Dr. Weiss leave as his gaze remained on that flashing sign. A plan stirred in his mind.

The colonel and his team were off on another mission, which meant members of his black ops team were either with him or taking possession of the control room. Now was the perfect time to see just what was in those boxes they had been removing.

Agent Hessman turned around to see an empty hallway and hurried towards the high-security storage room the colonel and his team had been using as their headquarters. He wondered where Mr. Thomas had gone.

CHAPTER 3
STEALING THE FUTURE

AGENT HESSMAN SET A BRISK pace down the hall, rushing past a sign labeling the section ahead as "restricted" to the high-security storage room the black ops team had been using. With the black ops team off on their own mission through time, the hall was empty.

Empty, except for one person waiting in front of the storage room door with her foot tapping. Agent Hessman approached her.

"I took a shortcut," Sue stated.

"I see we're both on the same wavelength with this thing. So, how come you didn't enter already, Sue?" Agent Hessman asked.

"Two reasons. One, if I go in with the head of base security, Cassidy can't accuse me of breaking any regs, and two, he's got his own private code on the lock."

Agent Hessman glanced at the door the two of them now stood before. It bore a simple sign: *Colonel Cassidy—Private*. In place of a doorknob or keyhole, the door had a number pad and retina scanner.

"I assume you have a way to get in?" Sue asked.

Agent Hessman reached for the number pad and faced the retina scanner. "In my capacity as head of base security, I installed back doors to every security device on the premises a long time ago." He pressed a sequence of numbers. A brief flicker of red light shone across his eyes, and the door slid open.

"And *that* would be why I waited," Sue remarked.

They stepped in together and scanned the room. It was empty but for a stack of grey boxes that almost reached the ceiling in the far corner. Metal boxes, each about a cubic foot in size. Each bore an electronic lock.

Sue knelt down for a brief examination of a box on the floor in front of the large pile. "I don't suppose you have a bypass code for *these* things?" she asked.

"He brought them in from off base, so unfortunately, no."

"Ah, possible contraband then." Sue grinned as she stood back up. "Do you mind if I try my own way of unlocking them?"

"Just don't forget to use a silencer," Agent Hessman said, stepping back. "I don't feel like getting deafened in a confined space by your 'key.'"

Without further ado, Sue pulled a pistol out of her belt, fitted a silencer to it, and took aim at the first box's lock. A muffled bang, and the lid popped open.

"Consider it unlocked," she stated.

As Sue re-holstered her weapon, Agent Hessman stepped over to the box and carefully reached inside.

"This feels rather familiar," he announced. He pulled out a pistol of a unique design not seen anywhere else and passed it up to Sue. As she turned it over in her hand, he pulled out some equally unusual bullets.

"Looks like the guns those Russians from the future had with them," Sue remarked.

"And their electrified bullets." Agent Hessman handed her one. "There are two more guns in here and a couple of cases of the bullets."

"Makes you wonder what's in all the other boxes." Sue tossed the futuristic pistol and ammo back into the box. She stepped over to another box and pulled out her own gun again. A few moments later, the next box was open, and she was pulling out what looked like a skinny hazmat suit.

"My, what unusual pajamas the colonel packs," she quipped as she held the suit up for examination. "You think he's got a pair of bunny slippers to go with it?"

Agent Hessman took the fabric in his fingers. It had a fine silk-like texture that was softer yet stronger than anything he had ever felt before, confirming what he already suspected. "That's one of the camo suits, alright," he stated. "Care to guess what sort of stuff is in all the other boxes?"

Sue dropped the suit, pulled out her gun, and cocked it. "Who's guessing?"

The third lockbox they opened contained pieces of unidentifiable equipment. One looked like a multimeter, but the dial was labeled with unknown symbols. Another appeared to be a simple metal cube an inch across. There was a disc that looked like an old CD but three times as thick, and another palm-sized cube, but this one had a single button on top.

"Be careful not to touch anything to trigger these things," Agent Hessman warned. "They could be anything from weapons to kid's toys."

Sue held the cube with the button, turning it over in hand. "I'm betting it's a kid's toy."

She showed him the bottom where was engraved some small print in English along with a logo. The print said, "Ken-Bee Toys."

"Nevertheless." Agent Hessman stood up and stepped back.

Sue tossed the mysterious cube back into the lockbox and looked over the pile as a whole.

Agent Hessman scanned boxes too. He could not imagine what future wonders were secured in them. "If Dr. Weiss is correct—"

"And when is he not?" Sue interjected.

"—then these thefts of future-tech could really backfire. General Karlson needs to know about this."

"I'll get a squad."

☾

Agent Hessman found the doors leading to Temporal Chamber Two had remained locked from the inside during the duration of Colonel Cassidy's recent excursion. When the doors finally swung open to the hallway, the colonel exited in the lead followed by the six black ops men in their jumpsuits. One of them carried another metal lockbox, this one about a third the size of the ones in the storage room. The colonel and his team got no more than a couple of feet down the hall when they were stopped by a row of guns aimed directly at them.

"What is this?" the colonel roared. "Stand aside immediately!"

The rifles, each held by a base security soldier, remained aimed at Colonel Cassidy and his squad. The general, Agent Hessman, Sue Harris, and many other staff, including Mr. Thomas, filled the hallway.

Agent Hessman and Sue Harris stood in front of the open lockboxes. To the left stood a perturbed-looking Dr. Weiss, Ben and Claire, along with Captain Beck, the large muscular man who had danced with Claire at her wedding, the meek-looking Mr. Thomas, and assorted base scientists and personnel.

The general stepped forward and glared at Colonel Cassidy.

Colonel Cassidy glanced at the open boxes, then back to the general. "I'm under orders," he stated. "Everything I've done has been under mission parameters and above your pay grade."

"Above our pay grade?" Dr. Weiss roared. "Colonel, you have no idea what you're dealing with! Aside from the fact that we have no idea how to use any of this, have none of the required system hookups, and would probably end up injuring someone trying to figure it all out, the cause-and-effect problems are enormous."

"May I remind you, doctor," the colonel replied levelly, "that one such item has cured your niece?"

"An example of time correcting itself from the damage that your future counterpart created in the first place," Dr. Weiss countered, waving his cane angrily.

Ben and Claire held him back, each holding him by a shoulder.

THE ALIENS STEP IN

"Easy there, Sam," Ben said. "While I'm sure the general might let you swing that cane, the colonel could fold you up in one of those boxes, and you know it."

Dr. Weiss relented with a grumble.

The general looked at the colonel and said, "Your activities are hereby suspended pending further investigation."

"You don't have the authority," the colonel countered. "My orders come straight from the Pentagon."

A soldier came running up the hall to Agent Hessman and whispered in his ear.

"Orders go through me first," the general barked.

"Not this time, General Karlson. I am—"

"General," Agent Hessman interrupted, "I've just been informed that we have lost all contact with the surface security team."

"That's my team," the colonel smugly grinned. "This entire base will soon be under my sole authority."

"We'll see about that," General Karlson snapped. "Lou, send someone up to see what's going on."

Agent Hessman nodded and pulled out his cell phone, stepping into a corner.

☾

"Your efforts are useless, General," Colonel Cassidy said.

"Colonel," Dr. Weiss fumed, "you have no idea the sorts of forces—"

"Who are you to talk?" the colonel snapped. "Professor Stein is married to someone who shouldn't even exist! That sounds like a pretty big temporal violation right there. At least I'm doing this for the good of my country instead of concern over some out-of-time gold digger."

Claire gasped at the remark, and her shock rippled through the personnel behind her.

"I won't have you speak that," The general said.

Sue narrowed her eyes at the colonel and clenched her fists.

"You mind if I borrow your cane for a bit, Sam?"

"It would be my honor," Dr. Weiss replied, handing Ben his staff.

"Even back in my time, back when I was a kid," a shocked Claire stated, "such a remark would have you on the field of honor, or at the least, facing—I think the modern term is—*a world of hurt*."

"Ben, you're no fighter," Sue said. "Allow me to be your stand-in."

"Granted," Ben grinned. He extended Dr. Weiss's cane to Sue. "This might even be fun to watch."

"Bring it," the colonel countered, "but when my people get down here, I'll have you all—"

"Hold it!" Agent Hessman shouted as he ended his phone call. The expression on his face brought everything to a halt. Everyone riveted their silent attention on him.

"There's nothing up there," he announced into the quiet.

"Probably," the colonel began, "because my backup—"

"No, I mean *nothing*," Agent Hessman explained. "No security, no buildings, no facilities, no nothing. The whole facility is just . . . gone."

The colonel looked at the confused expressions of everyone else.

Dr. Weiss appeared less puzzled and more urgently contemplative. "There can be only one possibility," he stated. "I must have a look at the detection grid."

Agent Hessman commented, "I think I know what you are thinking."

"Command center," the general ordered. "Now!"

"General," the colonel began, "may I remind you that—"

"Enough." The general turned to Agent Hessman. "Bring along the colonel and his people. Under guard."

☾

It was a quick march down the hall from Temporal Chamber Two to the command center, with the general and Dr. Weiss leading the way. Agent

THE ALIENS STEP IN

Hessman's security force kept their guns aimed at the colonel, whose six black ops team members found themselves caught with their weapons still holstered. The lockbox remained in the hands of the lead black ops member as everyone hurried down the hall.

"Turn on the detection grid," the general ordered.

"General Karlson," Colonel Cassidy tried once again, "turning the grid back on before my team has had a chance to clear any classified—"

Dr. Weiss rushed over to his station at the central dais and pressed the *on* button.

"If you mean you haven't had a chance to erase the evidence," the general snapped, "that's what I'm counting on. Agent Hessman, Sue—keep an eye on the colonel and his squad." The general stood beside Dr. Weiss, Ben, and Claire, and focused on the flickering screen.

The main screen lit up with its usual graphical displays, a series of lines appearing with time-marks labeling different sections, and then it came alive with speeding graphics, racing lines, and a world-map overlay.

"Sam, what are we looking at?" General Karlson asked.

"It's a temporal displacement wave, alright, and a big one," Dr. Weiss replied.

"Is it those Russians from the future again?" General Karlson asked.

"No," Dr. Weiss replied. "It looks like . . ."

One line arced across the main screen to land firmly in the middle of another large Asian country.

" . . . China," Dr. Weiss announced. "And from the look of the time codes, the event occurred exactly when the colonel's black ops team was out on their mission and had the grid down."

"The Chinese?" the general puzzled. "How'd they do it? Can you pinpoint what they changed to erase the rest of this facility?"

"Working on it." Dr. Weiss's fingers flew across his keyboard.

"The Chinese have been interested in getting their own time travel program off the ground," Agent Hessman said thoughtfully.

"Apparently it's further along than we suspected," Sue remarked.

"Obviously," said Dr. Weiss. "But what bothers me is the timing. There's only one way that China knew just when to strike . . . Sue, that Chinese exchange scientist—"

"Dr. Howard Ping," she concluded for him. "On it." Sue glanced quickly around the room, and then set a swift pace to a mapping station near Dr. Weiss.

Dr. Weiss turned to the general. "It looks like they've erased the entire American time travel program, which is why anything of the facility above ground isn't there anymore," he said. "We're only still around because of the temporal neutral field we installed. But that's only good for about twenty-four hours."

"Then we've got that long to figure out exactly what they did and fix it," General Karlson decided. "Sam, get on it. I want our main team out in fifteen minutes."

"Yes, General," Dr. Weiss snapped back.

"And Colonel Cassidy . . ." Grinning, General Karlson turned around to face the colonel and his squad. "You are obviously under house arrest. If you have to ask the charges, you haven't been paying attention."

In reply, the colonel growled.

"You can toss this guy into the same cell," Sue said as she approached with a firm grip on Dr. Ping.

"Our exchange scientist is an agent for the Chinese government," Agent Hessman announced.

"You have no proof," Dr. Ping replied. "If you do not release me, the diplomatic ramifications—"

"China knew exactly when to strike," Agent Hessman explained. "As short as the colonel's trips usually are, they would know down to the second when his team is readying to make a trip through time and also that our detection grid would then be off-line. Since the good doctor here is the only exchange scientist we have in from China—"

"Good enough for me," the general decided. "Lock him up along with—"

"I've heard enough."

Everyone in the room turned toward the doorway and the unexpected, authoritative voice. It came from a dark-haired man who had so far exuded the definition of averageness. This apparently meek and quiet person—Mr. Thomas—now displayed a more commanding demeanor with the look of a predator glittering in his eyes. He marched directly up to the dais toward the general, brushing past Sue with a paper in one hand and ID in the other.

He handed both paper and ID to the general. "I am Mr. Rutger Thomas, a special observer sent by the President and with *full* authority to do whatever may be necessary."

"*Rutger* Thomas?" The general remarked.

"Sounds like you've heard of this guy," Sue remarked to the general. "How bad, Lou?"

Agent Hessman simply nodded toward Colonel Cassidy.

General Karlson glanced at the colonel, who was now doing something he had never done previously, even when facing down the general.

The colonel was sweating.

CHAPTER FOUR
TAKING CHARGE

MR. THOMAS LOOKED FROM THE sweating colonel to the general who was glancing at Thomas's verification papers.

"Signed by the President himself," the general said, "with a special note for me and you, Lou." He handed Agent Hessman the paper and the ID.

Mr. Thomas smiled as though gloating.

Agent Hessman glanced at the documents and handed them back to Mr. Thomas. "It's legit," he announced. "Rutger Thomas himself. Known to many in certain circles by various nicknames, none of which I will repeat while in his presence."

"I am well aware of what people call me," Mr. Thomas snapped, "and if my reputation is one more tool to help me accomplish my mission, then so be it."

"Lou," General Karlson asked, "for the benefit of all present, perhaps you could give us a quick rundown of what you know of Mr. Thomas here?"

"In short, and with all due respect," Agent Hessman stated, "he's a no-nonsense problem solver who has worked for the last several administrations, sent in to do the dirty jobs that no one else can handle. He is

THE ALIENS STEP IN

rumored to have political connections, and on his last mission, he fired everybody and jailed nine people, including a general and a senator."

Claire leaned toward Ben. "He sounds more like a thug," she whispered.

"And," Mr. Thomas added, spinning around to face Claire and Ben, "I am possessed of excellent hearing."

Claire shrank into Ben's arms.

Mr. Thomas turned back to the general. "General Karlson, by the authority given me by the President, I am hereby taking charge of this base and all within it."

"Yes, sir," General Karlson replied.

Mr. Thomas continued. "Let me begin my role by stating how the whole lot of you messed things up. General Karlson and Special Agent Hessman should have been stricter with the colonel's group, no matter what level of pressure came down from the Pentagon. All of history is at stake, and that's just a bit out of the Pentagon's pay grade!" He turned to the still-sweating colonel. "And Colonel Cassidy, when a renowned scientist specializing in the field of temporal physics tells you that something is dangerous, you *listen* to him!"

"I had my orders direct from—"

"And you also have common sense and authority to use your own judgment," Mr. Thomas snapped. "I know because I read those orders before I came here. First, it was the stinking Cossacks from the future, and now, as a result of your foolishness and everyone else's incompetence, we have given the world's timeline to the mooks. I want to see this mess fixed up *now*. Got that?"

"Dr. Weiss," General Karlson replied, "with each trip the colonel's team made through time, they shut down the tracker so they couldn't be traced."

Mr. Thomas glared at Dr. Weiss.

"Correct," Dr. Weiss replied as he tightened his grip on his cane tightened and his face flushed.

"Regardless, Dr. Ping would have noticed each single time the tracker went down and been able to inform his people," the general continued.

"When you reclaim the backup temporal logs of the colonel's trips, check for signs of any additional temporal activity. Maybe this wasn't the first trip the Chinese made to the past."

"On it," Dr. Weiss replied. He returned to his work and began consulting with terminal technicians.

"And that brings us to Dr. Ping." As he said this, Mr. Thomas stepped across the platform towards Sue. Everyone moved out of his way as though he were Moses parting the Red Sea.

Sue released her steady grip on Dr. Ping and stepped aside, staying within arm's reach.

"You were acting as a spy, Mr. Ping, and you will be treated as one." Mr. Thomas reached into his coat pocket.

Ping straightened his back. "I am a representative of the People's Republic of—"

In one swift movement, Mr. Thomas pulled a gun from his pocket and aimed it at the spy's forehead from point-blank range.

Bang!

Mr. Ping's body thudded to the ground. Mr. Thomas stepped over it and crossed the room to where the colonel and his squad were still being held.

Colonel Cassidy glanced at the smoking gun in Mr. Thomas's hands but held his chin high.

"Then there's you, Colonel." Mr. Thomas put his gun away. "Your unit is hereby disbanded, and your former squad remanded to the custody of Special Agent Hessman's security personnel."

The colonel scowled. "When this is over, I'll simply take it up with—"

"Your rank is hereby reduced to *private*," he said sharply, "and you are to be held for court martial. As for your contact in the Pentagon, I plan to have General Izacks arrested for treason as soon as I have this current mess cleaned up." Mr. Thomas spun away from Private Cassidy to face Agent Hessman.

Agent Hessman motioned to his security personnel. They began pulling the former colonel and his squad out of the room, and one of them took possession of the lockbox the colonel's people had been holding.

"Special Agent Hessman," Mr. Thomas said, "everything that his squad brought back is hereby under quarantine. You are to go through those lockboxes and match it up to the catalogue that I am sure the black ops team kept and make sure that nothing is missing."

"Immediately," Agent Hessman replied. "Sue, get some people going on that. And take Ping's body out of here."

"That's just the preliminaries." Mr. Thomas marched toward the central dais. "I am going to launch an immediate investigation. Ping needed someone on the inside to get him the clearance and pass him through. He needed a cohort, and I will not stop until I find that cohort. As of right now, *everyone* is a suspect!"

During all this, Claire stood next to Ben, and everyone else tried to appear nonchalant. No one wanted to catch a direct gaze from the fearsome Mr. Thomas.

But one among them now stepped out, bravely putting himself in Mr. Thomas's path.

The man, Captain Beck, came to attention before Thomas and spoke. "I personally approved Dr. Ping's credentials."

"Bob?" the general asked, puzzled. "Did you not suspect that he could have been—"

"Oh, I knew," Captain Beck admitted. "I figured that what little he might learn would keep a sort of balance of terror going. This technology is not something that any one nation should have. But I assure you that I had no idea the Chinese were that far along, much less be able to attempt something like this. I figured at worse, they'd keep everyone cautious."

"I thank you for the confession," Mr. Thomas snapped, "but you are under arrest pending further investigation. Special Agent Hessman, lock him up."

Agent Hessman nodded. Disappointment came over Captain Beck's face as Agent Hessman let him away by the arm.

Dr. Weiss cleared his throat. "Mr. Thomas," he called with a tremor in his voice.

Mr. Thomas turned to face him. "Yes, Dr. Weiss?"

"Captain Beck's actions may not have been the wisest, but he's right in one thing. The Chinese shouldn't have been that far along."

"Then that gives us—and by that, I mean *you* specifically—something else to investigate," Mr. Thomas replied. "General Karlson?"

"Fifteen minutes, everyone," the general ordered. "We're really on the clock with this one."

Mr. Thomas glared at each person left in the room and they scurried to their duties.

CHAPTER FIVE
THE NEW MISSION

A PAIR OF THE COLONEL'S SECURITY guards stood at the door as Special Agent Hessman entered the storage room with the stack of open lockboxes on the floor. The unopened lockboxes were unceremoniously unlocked by Sue's favorite type of "key" and quickly examined. Sue would pull something out, identify it, and Agent Hessman checked it off a manifest currently displayed on a laptop confiscated from Colonel Cassidy's quarters.

"Looks like a brown coil," Sue said as she held up the next item.

"Check," Lou replied. "Good thing this catalogue of theirs has pictures, or I'd never know what a 'quantum oscillator' is supposed to look like. What else?"

"That's it. And that was the last box."

"Then we're in trouble, because we haven't found several listed items."

"Well then," Sue said as she stood up, "I guess we know who to talk to about that. You know, I've got a brand-new pair of good old brass knuckles I've been dying to try out."

"Should be fun to watch. Let's hurry. That meeting is in a few minutes,"

Agent Hessman said.

☾

Agent Hessman opened the cell door and allowed Sue to enter. He watched her brass-knuckled fist come solidly across Cassidy's chin, followed by her foot against his throat as he lay on the ground, face-up. Sue grabbed him by the collar and propped him up against the wall.

Agent Hessman held up the laptop and launched immediately into questioning. "According to your own manifest, there's a few items missing. Where are they... *Private* Cassidy?"

"And please make a fuss about answering," Sue said. "I still owe you for insulting Claire."

Holding his throat, Cassidy spoke in a raspy voice. "I'm just a soldier. I follow orders. We were to collect what we could and then everything along."

"To where?" Agent Hessman asked between tight lips.

"Some samples were already sent off to be studied by some scientists."

"In other words," Agent Hessman stated, "off base."

"Well then," Sue said, clenching her brass-knuckled hand, "while you're still conscious, you're going to tell us exactly where you sent them."

"That sounds like a threat," Private Cassidy grimaced. "In a fair fight, when I'm not on the ground with your boot pressed into my throat, we both know that I could easily take you."

Sue grinned as she raised her brass knuckles again.

☾

The drab conference room held only a long table and metal chairs. Mr. Thomas took his place at the head of the table as the entire team filled the room—minus Captain Beck, who was replaced by a new face with lieutenant's markings. The general sat to the right of Mr. Thomas while Agent Hessman sat with his laptop to the left of Mr. Thomas. Wearing a satisfied

THE ALIENS STEP IN

expression, Sue stood against one wall.

"Report," Mr. Thomas snapped.

"Before Private Cassidy had to be admitted to the infirmary, he confessed that some items had already been sent off to his people for study." Agent Hessman turned the laptop to face Mr. Thomas. "I have a list of the exact locations and names of people each of the missing items was sent to. We should be able to track them down just as soon as we've fixed our main problem."

Mr. Thomas scanned the laptop screen. A short list of names and addresses appeared, and alongside each, the designation of one of the missing items. He nodded curtly. "Knowing how these things work," he said, "they've probably passed into third-party hands by now. No matter; as soon as I'm able, I will have each of these people traced as well as anyone they've come in contact with."

Mr. Thomas closed the laptop and looked back up, turning to Dr. Weiss. "What do you think, Doctor?"

"The temporal trace leads right to where they could do the most harm," Dr. Weiss responded. "Back to the very first meeting of the three scientists who made time travel possible: Dr. Rick Fine, Dr. Nick Tes, and Dr. Isaiah Newly. Apparently, the Chinese did something to prevent them from meeting, thus preventing the development of time travel in this country."

"Then the new mission is obvious," General Karlson stated. "Go back to that meeting, discover what it was the Chinese did, and undo it."

"I would also point out that we must be extra cautious this time, though," Dr. Weiss warned. "In such a recent time period, and considering the location, some of us run a very real chance of running into our past selves."

"Can we simply do without any team members who might have that risk?" Mr. Thomas asked.

"I am afraid not," Dr. Weiss sighed. "That would include myself and Agent Hessman. Both of us are necessary for this mission."

"Then extreme caution must be exercised on your parts," Mr. Thomas agreed. "What about the other team members?"

"Yes," Ben responded politely. "I just wanted to say that despite the remarks of the former Colonel, my wife Claire has been a key component of these missions. In fact, if not for her unique insights—"

"Professor Stein," Mr. Thomas interjected, "Did I say anything about Claire not going? I've been through all the personnel files and am well aware of the unique contributions that your wife makes to these missions. In fact, I was going to insist that she go along. Now, to the rest of it. Dr. Weiss?"

Ben sat down, and Claire smiled at him. She cast an uncertain look at Mr. Thomas.

Pacing, Dr. Weiss read from his own electronic pad. "While the black ops team erased most of the logs, we were able to recover enough of them to find a few residual traces of some temporal incursions. Enough to know that it *was* China in each case. The visits were always brief, never enough to really do anything, but more like . . . I would say something in the way of a temporal mapping expedition."

"Explain," Mr. Thomas snapped.

Dr. Weiss stopped pacing. "Well, I would say they were test trips. To see what was possible and collect data, perhaps to complete some sort of program for their own time machine. I would even say that the only reason their last trip was so successful in changing our reality is because of the data they collected for their program during their past trips. My guess is they were mapping events in time that *can* be changed to some notable degree, or other ways in which their trips can be more successful."

"Wait a second," Ben said, "I thought you couldn't really change the significant points, just the small stuff."

"In essence, yes," Dr. Weiss replied. "But it may be that while many events are fixed points, there are some that can be shifted around a bit. For our case, what cannot be changed is the discovery of time travel itself, but the detail that *can* be shifted is *who* discovers and first uses it. The Chinese may have found a way to locate these temporal hinge-points during their past mapping expeditions. If this is true, that ability would heavily shift the balance of power to the Chinese and jeopardize our time travel facility."

"So, even if this change gets reversed," Agent Hessman said thoughtfully, "the Chinese will still have developed a way to make other significant changes as well."

Dr. Weiss nodded. "You are correct about the threat this poses. This last trip of theirs may have been the final proof of concept for their scientists. Even once we get things straightened out, they'll still have this new temporal technology. Once they have the specifics nailed down, it's all over for everyone; China will be able to change anything in history that they want to."

"Thank you, Dr. Weiss," Mr. Thomas said with a curt nod. "You have summed up the problem quite succinctly."

But Dr. Weiss remained where he stood.

"Was there something else?" Mr. Thomas asked.

"Well, yes there is. I'm not sure what to make of it, and it may still be of minor consequence . . ."

"In this investigation, Doctor, I consider *nothing* to be of minor consequence. Spit it out."

"Well . . . that is . . . I discovered something else in the logs. For lack of a better term, I might call it background noise. There's only a little bit of it with the first black ops trips, but it seems to increase with each later trip. I'm not sure what to make of it."

"Take an educated guess," Mr. Thomas said sharply. "Spare me nothing."

"If I had to guess, I would say some sort of temporal energy buildup from so much time travel."

"That definitely sounds like something significant to be aware of."

"Which would be why I mentioned it," Dr. Weiss said, still looking a little nervous. "But there is something else as well."

"The part I'm not going to like, I take it?"

Dr. Weiss nodded.

"Let's hear it."

Dr. Weiss wet his lips with his tongue and continued. "Mixed in with this background noise, I found what looks like a coded signal, but it appears to be coming from our present time while overlapping with the temporal distortion waves. I can't trace the origin, and while it's obviously intelligent, it doesn't match up to anything known."

"Might be another new surprise that the Chinese have come up with," General Karlson stated. "Have all technicians keep an eye out for any further evidence of that signal."

"Yes, sir," Dr. Weiss replied, returning to his seat.

"In the meantime," General Karlson continued, "we have something more important to get to."

"And what is that, General?" Mr. Thomas asked.

"As I see it, the mission is now two-fold. First, to prevent the change from happening while not getting seen by your past selves, and second, to discover whatever new time travel secret the Chinese have that's made this disaster possible."

"We might be able to use a couple of those camo suits the black ops team brought back from the future," Dr. Weiss interjected. "As near as we can tell, it's passive technology. You just put it on, and it works."

"I don't know . . ." the general hesitantly replied. "We may not know all the dangers."

"Will it help get the mission accomplished more efficiently?" Mr. Thomas asked.

"If they work as intended, then yes," Dr. Weiss replied. "At worst, they will not be a hindrance."

"Then do it," Mr. Thomas ordered. "Camo suits and some of those electronic stun guns, just in case."

"We've only got two suits and one stun gun," the general amended. He turned to Mr. Thomas. "As I am sure you will realize, we wish to minimize any more cross-temporal problems."

"Agreed," Mr. Thomas said with a curt nod. "Now, as for the team—"

"It will consist of myself, Professor Stein and his wife, Dr. Weiss, and

Lieutenant Frederick Polson," Agent Hessman said.

The lone lieutenant in the room stood up. Mr. Thomas looked Polson up and down. He appeared to be in his late twenties, a bit over six feet, with short blond hair, and a mound of muscle. "And why are you here?" Mr. Thomas asked.

"Lieutenant Polson is a Navy Seal," Agent Hessman said. "He will serve as the team muscle as needed."

"The muscle of the week," Claire quipped.

"Acceptable," Mr. Thomas stated.

"But regarding Captain Beck—"

"He will remain behind as I question him in your absence."

"Then the mission is a go," General Karlson announced. "Departure time is as soon as we get the time chamber warmed up."

A cell phone buzzed. The general pulled the phone from his pocket.

"Karlson here."

Mr. Thomas held his hands behind his back and waited, frowning, as the room fell silent. No one would dare interrupt the general during such an important meeting unless it was crucial.

A moment later, the general snapped his phone closed and glanced at Agent Hessman.

"Samantha is awake and asking for you, Lou."

Mr. Thomas appeared startled as he watched all eyes turn to Agent Hessman, who remained motionless. It seemed like forever to the man at the center of attention though it was only a second before he replied in his business-like manner: "This mission is more important than my personal life."

Not another word said, Agent Hessman stood up and set a brisk pace out of the room.

CHAPTER SIX
GETTING STARTED

SPECIAL AGENT LOU HESSMAN APPEARED outside the Pasadena Convention Center in California with the other time travelers—Ben and Claire, Dr. Weiss, Agent Harris, and Lieutenant Frederick Polson. He could not help but remember being in the same place seven years prior when he had led security for the important physics conference they were about to reattend.

On this occasion, the time travelers came out from behind a boarded-up restaurant in a mall across the street from the main building of the convention center. The facility was gigantic and appeared to be made of something resembling crystal. It bore a yellowish cast as if the construction material had some form of internal illumination. The same qualities appeared in the castle-like spirals surrounding the main structure.

From what Agent Hessman could see, the convention center was quite busy. Several squat buildings were scattered closely about the grounds. The central building had a staired entry leading down to basement levels and the bulk of the convention facilities.

"Okay, Sam, before we step one foot in any direction, what's the lowdown?" Agent Hessman asked.

"Well, the three scientists in question—Dr. Rick Fine, Dr. Nick Tes, and Dr. Isaiah Newly—first met at a physics conference being hosted by Jet Propulsion Laboratory right here at the Convention Center. They had contacted General Karlson to discuss some wild idea about time travel: the concept of temporal distortions and the ability to monitor time travel activity."

"You seem pretty well informed about this," Claire asked. "Were you at this conference?"

"As usual, Miss Hill—excuse me, Mrs. Hill-*Stein*—your reporter's instincts are on the money," Agent Hessman said. "The general did not come alone; he brought in his own expert on the subject, a top young scientist by the name of Dr. Sam Weiss."

"So, we're going to have to avoid meeting both your past self and that of General Karlson," Ben noted.

"And me," Agent Hessman interjected. "The general of this time period already knows me. Not to mention that I was in charge of security at this event."

"Then our solution presents itself," Ben pointed out. "We have two of those camo suits with us. It's only logical to put them on Lou and Sam here to make absolutely sure that neither are seen."

The suits in question had been folded into a small pack Sue carried, which she now proceeded to open.

"I must admit to being quite curious," Agent Hessman stated, touching the fabric. "And I admit to having my doubts. How safe are these things?"

As Sue held out one of the suits to Dr. Weiss, Lieutenant Polson grabbed it. "If there's a risk, then I should try it first, before you do, Dr. Weiss."

"Hey!" Dr. Weiss protested.

"You are far too valuable an asset to risk with untried technology, Sam," Sue said. "Besides, it would do nothing to hide your cane."

Dr. Weiss sighed like a disappointed child. "I suppose . . ."

Lieutenant Polson and Sue slipped on the bizarre suites. It was like stepping into the future.

Dr. Weiss took out a small electronic gadget about the size of an old hand calculator and started fiddling with it as he explained. "My portable time scanner has been upgraded to connect with the main system back in our own time, courtesy of a downlink through the wormhole. It effectively turns the scanner into a remote control. Not that it really controls anything, it basically interfaces with the main—"

"Sam," Agent Hessman cut in, "in five words or less."

"It's a time scanner," Sam shrugged. "With this, I can track any other time travelers in this time period, which currently would be us and the Chinese spies."

"Good," Agent Hessman said. "Everyone else, eyes up."

The second the Lieutenant and Sue closed up the last seam on their suits, they vanished from sight.

"Sam, it's you and me in the center. Ben and Claire, if you would, kindly walk in front of us to keep us from getting seen. Sue and Polson, how's it looking?" Agent Hessman asked.

Sue's voice came out from what seemed like thin air. "Operating fine so far."

"Just be careful of any shimmering effects," Agent Hessman warned. "That's how Samantha spotted the Russians."

"Affirmative," came Polson's voice.

Agent Hessman noticed a lot of people milling outside the main convention hall, some going down the stairs to subterranean levels. Several appeared to be of Chinese ancestry. But as he started to cross the street with Ben, Claire, and Dr. Weiss, he saw Claire's gaze turn toward the far right of the main building and hold there.

"Well, that didn't take long," Agent Hessman remarked. "Okay, Claire, what do you got?"

"Those two men over there." She nodded to indicate direction. "Their clothes are all brand new and excessively stylish."

"A lot of people are concerned about style," Ben pointed out.

"And nearly none of them are men," Claire replied. "And look how up-to-date their gear is, the fancy cameras they're using to snap all the touristy pictures. They're at least ten years ahead of this time and they're looking everywhere but at what they're taking pictures of. Their minds are clearly elsewhere. It's like they're foreigners trying way too hard to blend in with the crowds. And failing."

"Sam?" Agent Hessman asked.

Dr. Weiss aimed his time scanner in the direction of the two people in question, looked at the readout, and nodded. "It's two from the Chinese team, all right. And from what I can see, the object one of them is holding is *not* a camera."

"Time to move in," Agent Hessman ordered. "Keep it slow and casual. Harris and Polson, no swift moves in those untested suits . . . Harris? Sue? Polson?" When neither replied, Agent Hessman shook his head and sighed. "They're already moving in, aren't they? Okay, that's one point against those suits; can't keep track of anyone. Ben, you and Claire stay in front of me and Sam."

Agent Hessman and Dr. Weiss tucked their heads down, letting Ben and Claire lead the way. The suspicious Chinese men also seemed to be using the crowds to sneak into the convention center. The taller one discreetly looked at his palm—a handheld instrument, Agent Hessman surmised, very much like Dr. Weiss's time scanner.

With his chin down, Agent Hessman did what he could to survey the crowd for glimmers of Sue and Lieutenant Polson but saw nothing.

The four of them crept closer, doing their casual best to weave through the crowd so they could intercept the unsuspecting Chinese spies. Well-dressed people with plastic convention badges milled about, talking in clusters, as Agent Hessman's crew and the Chinese spies eased their way amongst them.

Then a flicker, a brief snap of ozone, and suddenly Sue and Polson materialized, causing three passersby to stumble, and startling the two Chinese spies, who were just a few yards away.

"Uh oh, their cover's blown," Agent Hessman noted.

The taller Chinese spy glanced at the time scanner in his palm and aimed it at Sue and Polson. He nodded at his companion, and then the pair ran away from Sue and Polson, who were pushing their way through the crowds toward them.

"So much for 'quietly,'" Agent Hessman sighed. "Just try not to make it look like a chase."

"A lady does not chase," Claire replied. "A lady pursues."

With a couple hundred people milling about, this pursuit would not be a fast-footed one.

CHAPTER SEVEN
THE FIRST CHASE

AS SHE RAN, SUE FLICKERED in and out of visibility like a bad light bulb. Polson had similar problems with his camo wear. Some people in the crowd rubbed their eyes as if they were seeing things.

"I knew there was a reason not to trust these things," Sue remarked. "Polson, I'll go for the spy with the gizmo. You hit the other."

"Right," Polson responded.

Meanwhile, the rest of the group seemed to be engaging in a pursuit that was not supposed to *look* like a pursuit. With Ben and Claire in front of Lou and Sam, the four of them made a more or less straight line for their quarry.

A man rushed through the crowds, bumping Claire to one side and Sam to the other. "Excuse me! I'm late!"

Agent Lou Hessman tried his best to push through the crowd and keep his quarry in sight. A few more collisions with the crowd, and he was certain only of one thing: he had lost everybody. Rather than continue his chase, he pondered where they might go.

A muffled sound caught Agent Hessman's attention. He turned in that direction and spotted another body floundering around in the crowd. It was Dr. Weiss, trying to weave his way through the mob. How could Agent Hessman determine which Dr. Weiss it was? The one from the future—the one he came with—or the one from this time?

Then he saw the cane in Dr. Weiss's hand.

Agent Hessman grabbed Dr Weiss by the wrist. Dr. Wiess spun around, ready to use his cane as a club—but he stopped short.

"Lou?" he asked.

"Yes," Agent Hessman replied. "And the right one." He pulled Dr. Weiss along silently.

When they were free of the crowds and listening ears, Agent Hessman spoke. "Let's get out of here before we get a visit from those time-traveling Chinese spies."

"Where to?" Dr. Weiss asked.

"Break out that remote scanner of yours and start plotting an interception course."

Dr. Weiss pulled out his time scanner.

☾

Agent Harris flickered her way along with Polson at her side. Under the unfamiliar fit of the camo suit, her vision limited by its hood, she tried to keep an eye on her targets.

"This is like running in galoshes fourteen sizes too large with a blindfold over one eye," she hissed to Polson. "Keep tabs on them for a minute."

Lieutenant Polson looked like a flickering stop-motion figure as he followed the faster-moving Chinese spies. Sue quickly surveyed her surroundings for any sign of cover. The corner of a building caught her eye, and she started an excruciating jog in its direction. For a suit made for stealth, the camo gear made her feel as though she stuck out like a turtle with a sluggish thyroid.

Around the corner, she ducked. Glancing quickly around to make sure

THE ALIENS STEP IN

she was alone, she started working at the top catch of her suit. A moment later her voice complained out of thin air, "And of course this thing doesn't have a normal zipper."

☾

Agent Hessman held the one electrified future gun the general had let him take back. It was loaded and aimed at the two Chinese spies. They took one look at it and stopped cold.

"Don't worry, it's only designed to stun," Agent Hessman stated. "Then we can have some quality *Q* and *A*." He pulled the trigger. Nothing happened.

The Chinese spies grinned and charged at him. The short one leaped at Agent Hessman's feet, the tall one at his upper body. Agent Hessman jumped over the short one and crashed straight into the tall attacker with a solid punch to his gut. As he and the tall attacker landed on the ground, Agent Hessman ducked a counter blow and replied with a punch to the tall man's face. That gained him enough time to leap to his feet and face off against the shorter one again.

The tall man rolled back up to his feet.

Agent Hessman pulled the trigger again, and once again, nothing happened. "Lousy piece of—"

As the short Chinese spy drew back his arm for another punch, Agent Hessman quickly flipped the gun around in his hand and swung it like a club. The butt end of his gun slammed into the side of his opponent's head, stopping the incoming punch.

The short man dropped immediately.

Agent Hessman glanced at his gun. "I guess this thing's good for something after all."

"Sa!"

Agent Hessman spun around to see his remaining opponent towering over him in a determined martial arts stance.

Agent Hessman sighed. "Just make it quick," he stated.

It was indeed quick. A karate chop came down with swift ferocity to the back of a neck—but the chop came to the back of the short Chinese spy's neck. As Hessman's opponent dropped, a large bulky cloth wrapped around the spy's head from behind and was pulled tight.

Agent Hessman looked up. "Thanks, Sue. We were wasting enough time."

"Found a use for the suit," she remarked.

The cloth with which she held the muffled Chinese spy was her camo suit. Behind her, Lieutenant Polson flickered into view as he stepped out of his camo suit.

Dr. Weiss emerged from behind the cover of the building. "Is it all over with?" he asked.

Agent Hessman stepped past the short assailant to the one struggling against Sue's hold. "This future pistol makes a passable club but not much else, I'm afraid," he stated. "Soon as the fight is out of that one, we'll get into some determined questioning."

Agent Hessman heard scuffing and spun around to see the tall spy make a weaving getaway around the corner.

"I'll get him!" Lieutenant Polson broke into a run.

"That's what the muscle's supposed to be for," Agent Hessman remarked. "Me? I'm supposed to be the investigator." He turned a determined eye now toward the short spy muffled by Sue's camo suit and jabbed a finger into his chest. "And I *always* get my answers . . ."

CHAPTER EIGHT
QUESTION TIME

AGENT HESSMAN LOOKED AT THE captive who was still flat on the ground as Sue tied his hands behind his back with a spare handkerchief.

"The suit was a bust, so I decided to go back to basics," she said.

"The gun didn't work either," Agent Hessman remarked. He turned to Sam. "Figure out why our toys from the future failed to work while I interrogate this guy."

Dr. Weiss nodded. He picked up the camo suit and future gun for a more careful examination.

Agent Hessman sat down on top of their startled captive who was flush after the chase. He drove his knee hard into the man's chest. "Now, you're going to tell me what brings you out here like this. What's the nature of your new tech?" When he received nothing but a defiant look, Agent Hessman pummeled his knee deeper into the man's chest. The result was a quiet cry and incomprehensible babble of Chinese.

"I'd advise you to cooperate, or I might let Sue here engage in her favorite hobby."

Once again, the spy offered a defiant look and a few choice words in

Chinese.

"He's not going to cooperate. Let me work him over. Just one hand, please?" Sue begged Agent Hessman.

"Agent Harris, I think I indulge you a little too much. The last one I let you work over nearly bled to death before we could get anything out of him," Agent Hessman said.

"But he talked, didn't he? Come on, just one hand? A finger?"

When still no response came from their prisoner, Agent Hessman stood up with a nod to Sue. "If he spoke a lick of English, that bit would have had him insulting us at the least."

To a few more words in Chinese, Sue reached down and slugged their captive; he would be napping for a while to come.

Agent Hessman turned around to see Dr. Weiss kneeling on the ground with the useless pistol and camo suit spread out before him. "What's the news?" Agent Hessman asked.

Lou and Sue gathered around Dr. Weiss as he knelt on the ground fiddling with the pistol.

"There appears to be a sensor pad on the gun's trigger. I'm guessing it's designed to work much like a fingerprint scanner, though more likely is a genetic scanner. If you don't have the registered genetic code, it won't work."

"A logical enough precaution," Sue remarked. "What about the suit? That thing was flickering pretty wildly."

"The camo suit must rely on some sort of active matrix," Dr. Weiss replied, pulling it closer. "And that requires power."

"So, the batteries ran out?" Agent Hessman asked.

"And replacement batteries are about a hundred years in the future. Heck, they could be woven into the fabric for all we know."

"Count on it," Agent Hessman sighed. "That's what would be most convenient for them and the most troublesome for us."

He turned away, thoughtfully pacing, then stopped. He glanced at their unconscious prisoner, then to the camo suit Lieutenant Polson dropped before he gave chase, and then back to the prisoner.

"We have a captive who can't talk simply because he doesn't know the language, and future tech that won't work . . . time to solve one problem with the other. Sue, gather up both suits and the gun."

While Sue did so, Agent Hessman fished around in the unconscious Chinese spy's pockets. His search was rewarded by a palm-sized circular object with a button—a familiar-looking beacon that would return the prisoner to his own time travel facility. "Roll up the camo suits and empty the ammo from the gun," Agent Hessman ordered.

Sue handed over the gun and the two folded camo suits. Agent Hessman placed the gun into one of the captive's pockets and the two folded camo suits on top of his stomach. Then he put the beacon on the man's chest. As Agent Hessman stood up, Sue reached down to slug the spy one more time. Then she pressed the button on the beacon and stepped away.

The man and the suits piled on top of him flickered and then dissolved in an explosion of rainbow lights.

Only once he vanished from sight did Sue ask the obvious question. "Any particular reason we just did that? They got the future tech now."

"The suits are useless and just weighing us down," Agent Hessman replied as Dr. Weiss came up to join them. "And as for the gun"—he opened Sue's hand to display the electronic bullets she still held after emptying the gun—"it's useless without the ammo."

Agent Hessman pocketed the ammo as he continued. "Of course, the Chinese operatives don't know this, so that should give them something to do for a long while as they try to figure it out."

"I would say there's a chance those items may not even reach them," Dr. Weiss said.

"Explain," Agent Hessman demanded.

"Simple. Once those items are back in the time corridor, there is a chance that they might simply snap back to where they belong. I'm really not sure, though."

"If that was true," Sue asked, "then wouldn't Claire have snapped back to her own time the last time she time traveled?"

"Like I said, I'm not sure. In her case, she was about to die so that may have made a difference. Or perhaps she really does belong in our time. We know so little that much of such conjecture is more in the realm of philosophy and not science."

"Save it for later," Agent Hessman decided. "Right now, we're on a mission." He glanced briefly around at their surroundings. They were behind a building that looked like some sort of factory and out of sight of the crowds that were milling about nearby. A pleasant day, perfect for a convention, though that made it much more difficult to track someone down.

"Next step," Agent Hessman stated, "we need to find Polson and see if he's caught the tall guy. Did anyone see which way Ben and Claire went off to?"

"We all got separated in the crowds," Dr. Weiss replied. "I'm only lucky you found *me*."

"Then that's something else on our list. Keep an eye open for them but remember to keep in mind that both Sam and I have past selves hanging around here," Agent Hessman advised.

"That could get confusing," Dr. Weiss realized. "When you pulled me from the crowds, I couldn't be sure which 'you' it was at first."

"Code phrases," Sue decided. "If one of us says . . . 'purple pimpernel,' then the other responds with 'no, it was orange.'"

"A rather odd choice of words," Dr. Weiss remarked.

"That's the whole point," Sue explained. "How often are you going to see that particular collection of words come up at random?"

"I see your point," Dr. Weiss said. "Very well. 'Purple pimpernel' and 'no, it was orange.' Got it."

"Then let's get marching," Agent Hessman told them. "And try to stay within sight of each other this time."

After a careful look around the corner to make sure the coast was clear, Agent Hessman let Sue take the lead. He and Dr. Weiss kept to the shadows.

CHAPTER NINE
THE CHINESE DEVICE

AGENT HESSMAN CAUGHT UP WITH Lieutenant Polson, who had the second Chinese agent on the ground. Almost immediately Claire, Sue, Ben, and Dr. Weiss arrived.

"Great job, Lieutenant," Agent Hessman stated. He bent down to examine the unconscious man's body and quickly located his beacon. When Agent Hessman reached into the left inner pocket of the man's jacket, he pulled out a strange looking device with unfamiliar dials and brightly colored triangular buttons on the side.

"Hand me that device. I think that is what we may be looking for," Dr. Weiss said.

Agent Hessman gave the strange device to Dr. Weiss. Then he placed the beacon on the Chinese agent's chest and slapped the button, backing away as the traveler disappeared in a flash of light.

Dr. Weiss examined the device. "This is amazing and appears to be what we're looking for. The display is in Chinese, of course, but from the types of waveforms it's displaying and the nature of the other controls, this appears to be a temporal data recorder. In fact, it might function much like

#1 – Chinese Temporal Data Recorder

THE ALIENS STEP IN

our own remote and link to equipment back in their own time through their wormhole."

"Get as much out of that thing as you can, Dr. Weiss," Agent Hessman said. "That device is key to this whole mission."

"Give me a few minutes." Dr. Weiss stepped away to examine the temporal data recorder in more detail while putting some distance between him and Sue as she kept lookout.

Agent Hessman faced Ben and Claire. "So, where did you two disappear to?" he asked.

"Lost at first," Ben admitted.

"But then I had to pick up a little trinket." Claire produced an envelope stamped with the Pasadena Convention Center logo and a signature scrawled across it. "Remember, I promised myself that I'd pick up a memento from each time period I traveled to. A nice African American gentleman named Neil signed it for me."

"Fine, I'm sure," Agent Hessman began, "but we still have a mission to—"

"Neil deGrasse Tyson, if that rings any bells," Ben finished for her. "The physicist?"

Agent Hessman paused, shaking his head.

"He was more talkative than the one in the wheelchair, poor man," Claire sighed.

"Scientist in a wheelchair? Do you mean Stephen Hawking?" Agent Hessman asked.

"That's the one," Claire replied.

Agent Hessman wondered how many other famous people Claire had encountered in her time travels. "We still have an unknown number of Chinese time travelers to find and a very limited time in which to do it," Agent Hessman said. "So, if you don't mind—"

"Right," Claire replied as she carefully tucked the signed envelope away. "Back to business."

"Sam," Agent Hessman asked, "how's it going with that thing?"

Dr. Weiss stepped back to rejoin them, still poking around at the display on the temporal data recorder in his hand. Sue stepped over a little closer as well, though still observing their surroundings. Lieutenant Polson kept a discreet watch by the corner of the building.

"Well," Dr. Weiss began, "this gadget is definitely designed to track and collect temporal readings, but it seems to work in conjunction with one or two other units."

"To triangulate?" Ben asked.

"Exactly. Which gives us something to work with."

"If they're all synced together," Agent Hessman ventured, "then can you use that to track down any others?"

"Exactly. That's what I'm working on right now," Dr. Weiss replied, his fingers moving about the controls. "I should also be able to use it to mess with their data. Change their input."

"I say we destroy it. That thing destroys our present, so get rid of it right now." Sue reached for the temporal data recorder in Dr. Weiss's hand.

Agent Hessman grabbed her wrist. "Destroy that, and the Chinese will simply make more. But if we can feed it false data, get them to believe that their project's failed—Sam, can you operate that thing?"

"I already have the basic functions figured out," Dr. Weiss replied. "It shouldn't be much longer before I can . . . Now there's a familiar looking wave pattern."

"Something we should be concerned about?" Ben asked.

"Possibly," a distracted Dr. Weiss replied. He worked a couple more controls, then frowned at what came up on the display, a messy mix of complex waveforms. "This thing is picking up the same temporal background noise that we saw back in the control room, only now it's a whole lot worse."

"What does that mean for our mission?" Agent Hessman asked.

"I'm not sure, but nothing good. If I had to guess, I'd say that if we don't complete this mission and fix the time stream, we might be in for something much worse than our disappearing time travel program. I'm surprised our Chinese colleagues didn't notice it, or maybe they did and took it as a sign of impending success for their mission."

"Sam," Ben said, "if that thing's triangulating with the others, do you think you could use it to get some more data on that background noise? I got a really bad feeling about that."

"I should be able to. Give me a moment."

Agent Hessman leaned in closer, frowning, as Dr. Weiss fiddled with the device's controls. The display on the small screen exploded into a chaotic mess of waveforms. Suddenly, one of them resolved down to something a lot more coherent.

"That looks like a signal of some sort," Sue noted.

"Good eye," Dr. Weiss replied. "In fact, it looks like that same coded signal we picked up back at the base. Its origin appears to be back in our own time, though, and . . ."

Another control turned and the display altered to something even more puzzling for Dr. Weiss.

Agent Hessman asks. "What's happening Dr. Weiss?"

"A coded signal, all right. One with a temporal carrier wave, if I read this thing right."

"A what?" Agent Hessman asked. "How is that possible?"

"I have no idea," Dr. Weiss admitted. "It's definitely very unusual."

"Well, as concerning as that is, we need to save it for later," Agent Hessman decided. "Feed them false data through that thing."

"On it." Dr. Weiss continued to fiddle with the data recorder.

Agent Hessman quickly glanced around as he considered their next move. Hundreds of people milled about the general area, each of them waiting their turn to go inside to what would become a conference of greater importance than any of them would have suspected.

"We need to figure out a way to get inside that conference," he stated. "We need to get to those three scientists."

"Oh, that," Claire shrugged. She reached into a pocket, and with her face beaming, pulled out a fistful of tickets.

"Tickets?" Agent Hessman said, an eyebrow raised in surprise.

"Girl, I know you got your ways," Sue remarked, "but how on God's green earth did you do it?"

"It was Ben, really," Claire replied. "While I was talking to Mr. Tyson and getting his autograph, Ben was at the ticket counter."

"The conference was selling observer tickets to members of the Planetary Society, of which I happen to be a member," Ben explained. "So, I only needed to show my pass. I had not attended this conference, nor was I in this part of the country at the time, so I was safe."

"And no one on the planet even knows my face," Claire interjected.

"Because this is only seven years before our time," Ben continued, "my money is still good. I simply bought us each a ticket. Paid for in cash. Want one?"

For a moment Agent Hessman was struck silent. Then a wide grin stretched across his face as he took one of the tickets from Claire's hand. "Remind me to include you in my report after this is done. Okay, we just became convention attendees. Sam, keep messing with that device. Sue, Polson, keep an eye out for our past counterparts. Let's get moving."

A ticket for each, they walked around the corner directly to the convention center entrance.

CHAPTER TEN

GETTING IN

AGENT HESSMAN WAS JUST APPROACHING the stairs that led down into the bowels of the convention center when Polson abruptly pushed him into the hallway. Sue nodded at Polson and ushered Dr. Weiss into the hallway after them, followed by Ben and Claire.

"It's Weiss and the general," Ben told them. "Past selves, of course."

"Good work, Polson," Agent Hessman said. "What are they doing?"

"From what I can tell, sir, they're just hanging around the entrance," the lieutenant replied.

"Sam," Agent Hessman asked, "I don't suppose you recall just how long you and the general hung out front before going in, do you?"

Dr. Weiss looked up from the temporal data recorder. "Huh? Oh. We waited out front until the general's security team certified the place safe for him. I guess that would have been you. I recall chatting with him about the people I was supposed to meet, but not for how long. Sorry."

"Then we need to find another way in," Ben said. "A back entrance, perhaps?"

"Not the way I had the place sewn up tight," Agent Hessman said. "As little time as we have, we may simply need to wait them out."

"Disguises," Claire beamed.

"What? No. I don't do disguises."

"You may have to," Sue pointed out. "Even once we're inside, there's still a risk of encountering them."

"I suppose you're right," Agent Hessman agreed. "Okay then, disguises for me and Sam, but how? That's part of a spy's skill set, not security's."

"Oh, men," Claire said with an eye roll. "Never prepared for what counts."

"And you are." Sue grinned.

Claire pulled a silvery-colored compact from her purse and snapped it open to reveal a range of powder and cream makeup colors. "You carry a full makeup kit with you?" Agent Hessman remarked.

"I'm from the year nineteen-nineteen, and I'm a woman," she replied. "Of course, I carry a full kit with me. Now just hold still, and in a few minutes, no one will recognize you at all."

"But lipstick and blush," Agent Hessman said in mild protest. "I don't want to look like a clown."

"Don't worry, Lou." Claire rubbed something flesh-colored onto Hessman's face.

"Ben, Polson; keep an eye on the old versions of Dr. Weiss and me," Agent Hessman said. "Pretend you're having a conversation and blend in."

Ben and Polson stepped to the front of the hallway, blocking Agent Hessman and the women, and they faced each other as if in conversation.

Sue tugged at Agent Hessman's jacket. "You've worn this thing too many times around the base and I'm guessing it's at least seven years old. Someone at the convention is bound to recognize it."

"Not much I can do about that," Agent Hessman replied. "How do I disguise my jacket?"

"By wearing it inside out."

"But it's not reversible."

"It is now. Come on, off with the sleeve."

THE ALIENS STEP IN

Claire dabbed her brush into another color. "A little contour below the cheekbones to make them look sunken, then some misplaced eyeshadow to give you the appearance of bags, and we'll have you looking like a stranger before you know it."

Agent Hessman sighed as Claire brushed one color after another over his face. He studied Dr. Weiss, whose expression showed growing concern.

Ben turned to Agent Hessman. "Past Weiss is engrossed in his discussion while the past general is looking impatiently at his watch and down towards the entry stairs. Doesn't look like he wants to be hanging around for very long," Ben remarked. "How you girls doing back there?"

"Just fine," Claire replied. She looked at Sue. "Now mess up his hair more. Brainy types never comb their hair right. They're either bald or look like they used a lawn rake to comb through their hair."

"One Cal Tech haircut coming right up," Sue replied. She ruffled her hands through Agent Hessman's hair, and he resisted the urge to smooth it back down.

Sue frowned. "Nope. Doesn't work. Now he looks like a homeless man. Let's smooth out a few strands."

While Sue fluffed his hair again, Claire brought another brush of color to his face.

"Just . . . about . . . right." Claire stepped back a foot for a more studied look at her creation. "Now, what else?"

"Looks good," Sue said. "His eyes look like they have bags, his cheeks are a bit sunken, and that scowl makes him look old. Really old."

"Just one thing missing," Claire decided. "That hair is way too young for the rest of him."

"Still the hair?" Sue asked.

"We don't have time for me to get a dye-job, girls."

"No need." Claire reached into her purse and pulled out a small bottle of talcum powder, straight out of 1919, which she tossed to Sue. "Give his hair a good dusting. Say about, two decades worth."

"On it," Sue replied.

Sue rubbed small handfuls of talcum powder through Agent Hessman's hair. After a final fluff and combing through it with her fingers, she dusted off his clothing.

"Not a day under sixty," Sue decided.

"Good job," Claire beamed. "Lou, just remember to walk with a stoop or something."

"The things I do to get a job done," Agent Hessman sighed. "Now what about Sam here?"

Dr. Weiss still had his nose in the Chinese device, nearly oblivious to the world around him.

"Let me take a look at the past Dr. Weiss," Claire said, stepping out of the hallway for a moment.

"Well, Past Dr. Weiss doesn't have a cane, so that's something different. He combs his hair neater than he does now, apparently, and he is not nearly as pale looking as he is now. Sam, you need to get out in the sun more."

"What?" Dr. Weiss looked up. "Oh, I guess I do, but ever since the time travel thing started, I've nearly constantly locked myself away with my projects."

"Well, for our purposes right now, it works," Claire decided. "You look totally different than you did seven years ago. You even have a little bit of grey creeping in around your temples that you didn't have back then." She gave Dr. Weiss's hair a light toss and clicked her tongue. "There. Just remember to keep your head down and use that cane like you really need it."

Dr. Weiss nodded and returned to studying the data recorder.

"Well, my job's done," Claire decided.

"Wait a second," Agent Hessman grumbled. "I get the full treatment, powder tossed in my hair, layers of makeup caked on me that I'll be spending hours washing off, and all he gets is a hand through his hair and a warning to stoop more?"

"Sorry," Claire shrugged. "Sam's changed a lot more in the last seven years than you have."

"The price you pay when you don't age in the time travel business," Sue quipped.

Agent Hessman scowled, but long years of self-discipline drew him back to the task at hand. "Okay, whatever works for the mission. Now, is everyone ready? When the next big crowd goes in, we slip in too. Just give your tickets—don't say a thing—and once inside we can start tracking down the rest of the Chinese team. Sam, how's it going on tracking them?"

Dr. Weiss kept his eyes on his gadget.

"Sam?" Agent Hessman repeated.

Ben lightly prodded Sam.

"Huh?" Sam looked up.

"We're ready to track the Chinese," Agent Hessman reminded him. "Use that gizmo you got there in your hand. You said that it could—"

"Oh yes, that," Dr. Weiss said with a faint nod. "Yes, between using this to locate their other temporal triangulation devices and our own remote for locating time travel signatures, I should be able to easily locate every single one of them."

"Should be?" Agent Hessman asked. "I thought that's what you were working on. Sam, we have very limited time to complete a very important mission."

"Agreed, but more important than we all first knew."

"Why does this sound like something I'm not going to like?" Sue sighed. "Ben, you wanna take the lead on this one?"

"Sam, what are you talking about?" Ben asked. "You already told us about the danger of the Chinese experiments with that temporal background noise. How much worse can it get?"

"Dear," Claire said to her husband, "I may be from nineteen-nineteen, but even I know that you never ask a question like that."

The physicist took out his own remote unit from one pocket and held it in hand alongside the Chinese device.

"I am afraid that it is a lot worse than even I feared," he began. "While examining this device, and using our own data coupled with some readings I got from our systems via the live-feed we have through our wormhole, not to mention my own temporal theories—"

"Sam?" Agent Hessman said with a nearly pleading look. "I just went through makeup hell that's given me more respect for how on earth women managed to do it all in so short a time, so I'm not in the mood for lengthy dramatic lead-ins."

"Oh, well, sorry about that. Great job on the makeup, though. You look years younger. Anyway, it all suggests that the Chinese theory is correct; they can change time under certain limited and very specific conditions. Not like *Back to the Future*, but possibly more like *Twelve Monkeys*. Or maybe—what's that Christopher Reeves time travel flick—*Somewhere in Time*? No, *Final Countdown* would be more like it."

"Sam," Agent Hessman snapped. "To the point!"

"Well, as I was saying, you can change certain unfixed events in time but doing so will cause vibrations in the time-space continuum. Like gravity waves, only through time."

"Is that the temporal background radiation we've been picking up?" Ben asked.

"Precisely," Sam stated. "Call them 'chronons' if you will. Each alteration of an event in time causes another release of these chronons."

"This is sounding like a temporal equivalent to radiation poisoning," Agent Hessman mused. "Is that what we're in danger of getting?"

"Oh no, it's *much* worse than that. You see, too much of this chronon build-up could create a sort of temporal black hole, the presence of which would collapse major segments of the timeline down around them. The result would be devastating. You'd have holes in time and space, which would cause devastation the likes of which I can't even imagine. Lou, they must be stopped from developing this technology of theirs."

"That," Claire remarked licking her lips, "sounds like Armageddon."

"Or worse," Ben added.

"In fact"—Dr. Weiss held up the Chinese device—"I've found a function in this unit that seems able to measure the same temporal background radiation we found on the equipment back home, and it shows radiation is on a drastic rise. If it continues at this rate, then we could be facing one such temporal black hole before this mission is even up. Lou, we must stop them at any cost."

"Got it," Agent Hessman stated. "Sue, Polson; kill order is authorized. If we have to send those Chinese back in body bags to save the world, then we do so."

"Affirmative," Lieutenant Polson replied.

"Then let's get moving," Agent Hessman continued. "Suddenly, the possible risk of discovery is well worth the alternative."

"But Lou, that's not what has me concerned."

Agent Hessman's jaw tightened. Polson turned away from his post, and everyone drew close to Dr. Weiss.

"It took the bulky scanning equipment in the control room to pick up that radiation. This"—Dr. Weiss held up their own remote—"is only an uplink to those scanners. But this"—he now held up the Chinese unit—"picks up that radiation all by itself. And it's a handheld unit. Such technology does not exist anywhere on this planet."

"Maybe the Chinese made a technological leap," Claire suggested.

"Not unless that leap involved about ten generations of development. This device of theirs should not exist."

Spinning thoughts and confusing realities robbed Agent Hessman of words. He studied Dr. Weiss's temporal radiation detector as they approached the stairwell. Two new blips suddenly appeared. Agent Hessman looked up to see two Chinese agents charging out of the stairwell towards them—perfectly matching the blips on Dr. Weiss's screen.

But the Chinese agents were not running after someone; they were running away from someone. Three security guards were hot on their heels.

CHAPTER ELEVEN
DOUBLE CHASE

"**I'M GUESSING OUR CHINESE ASSOCIATES** just ran afoul of security," Sue surmised. "Lou, do you remember any of this happening to you back in the past?"

"Yes. But that encounter has a whole lot more meaning now," Agent Hessman replied.

"Then this is our hinge-point," Ben observed. "It may be that they managed to escape security and still finish the mission that changed our present."

"Then we get to them first," Agent Hessman decided. "But watch out for our past selves."

"We'll use the code phrase," Sue reminded them.

"Code phrase?" Claire asked.

"Purple pimpernel," Sue quickly explained. "The counter is 'no, it was orange.'"

"Got it," Claire replied.

Sue pointed at the two Chinese men who were quickly weaving their way through the crowd. They were heading for an older structure that

THE ALIENS STEP IN

appeared to be part of the security system for the Convention center. "Go left, Polson, and I'll go right," she commanded. "We can trap them."

Sue and Polson shot away.

"Sam," Agent Hessman said, "you and I will have to go around back to avoid our past selves."

Dr. Weiss kept his eyes on the temporal radiation detector and offered a vague grunt.

☾

Sue headed toward the two Chinese time travelers who were attempting to return to the basement from which they had emerged. Lieutenant Polson steamed like a freight train toward the pair. When they saw the large Navy Seal approaching, the Chinese stopped short and turned around, shooting outside and away from both Polson and the three security guards who had tailed them out of the basement.

Sue broke into the fastest run she could manage, slipping behind one security guard and quickly working out an intercept course. She spotted another structure just ahead, one that appeared to be an old-style opera house. While the Chinese were playing bumper cars in their attempts to escape the security guards and Lieutenant Polson, she made a beeline for the front steps of the small opera house.

As predicted, once the Chinese time travelers had circled past the three security guards and outdistanced Polson, they headed straight for the opera house too. Sue leaped in front of them and landed on the first steps in a martial arts battle stance.

The short and tall Chinese men spun away from her to face the three security guards—one of whom, the man in the lead, was Agent Hessman. But this Agent Hessman wasn't covered in makeup, and he looked much younger than the Agent Hessman Sue had traveled back in time with.

"You can either make it easy on yourselves," Sue said to the Chinese men, "or you can give me the workout I've been needing."

"Who the hell are you?" Past Agent Hessman demanded of her.

Before she could respond, the two Chinese spies ran off to Sue's right and headed along the front of the next building with Past Agent Hessman and his security guards on their heels.

Polson, meanwhile, was tangled in a crowd of convention goers.

As they cleared the crowded convention entrance, the two Chinese swung left and made a dead run for a bus that was pulling to a stop before a cluster of waiting passengers. Past Agent Hessman followed with his men. Sue ducked behind a tree so Past Agent Hessman wouldn't wonder who she was again or why she was chasing them too.

The pair of Chinese time travelers leaped onto the bus as the door began to close.

Now what are they up to? Sue wondered. As the bus pulled away, she surveyed the street separating the mall and the convention center. The bus was heading straight past the facilities. It would pass a neighboring parking structure and come to a corner at the end of the block—where another bus stop was located.

Sue's eyes narrowed on that stop. "Looks like I get that workout after all."

Sue bolted after the bus just as Lieutenant Polson caught up to her. She pointed toward the next bus stop, and the pair of them picked up speed.

The bus stopped at the corner, with Past Agent Hessman and his men a dozen strides away. The two Chinese spies from the future tumbled out of the bus as the angry tone of the bus driver trailed after them. "Come back when you can actually pay the fare!"

As the Chinese men started to run back toward the convention center, dodging the crowds, Past Agent Hessman and his men stumbled through the throngs of people and tried to follow.

☾

Meanwhile, Claire, Ben, and Dr. Weiss were strolling through the convention center crowds toward the corner bus stop that the two Chinese spies were vacating. The men were heading straight toward them, and they were now less than a block apart.

"Sam, do me a favor," Claire suggested.

"What? Oh, sorry, I'm still working on this mechanism. What can I do for you?"

Claire stood on her tiptoes as if straining to see something through the crowds. "Could you snap your cane out at about a forty-five-degree angle?"

"What? But why?"

"And make it pretty hard," Ben added. "Right about . . . now."

"Huh? Well, okay." With a shrug, Dr. Weiss snapped out his cane—and the two Chinese spies tumbled over it.

"You can go back to your tinkering now," Claire casually remarked.

"What? But did I hurt someone?"

"Only the bad guys," Ben told him.

"Then shouldn't we be going after them?"

Claire nodded toward Sue and Polson, who were barreling toward them. "I'm a reporter, you're an absent-minded professor, and Ben is definitely not the physical type . . . well," she added with a quick smile for her husband, "mostly. We'll leave it to Sue and Mr. Muscles."

"I believe what we did is called marking the prey," Ben smiled.

"Quite so," Claire replied. "Now, shall we?"

Ben stuck out his elbow, which Claire took in hand, and the two resumed their strategic stroll away from the convention center with Dr. Weiss, who remained a step behind them, still puttering with the temporal radiation detector.

Claire glanced over her shoulder to see the two Chinese men continue through the crowd back toward the convention center, the tall man now handicapped by a notable limp.

One of the security men broke through the crowds and came up to Claire. "Excuse me, Miss."

Claire stopped. It was Agent Hessman, but a few years younger than the one she knew, sans makeup. Fortunately, Dr. Weiss's attention was buried in the device, his gaze lowered. For added protection, Ben and Claire closed in around him, shielding him from Past Agent Hessman's view.

Claire smiled at Past Agent Hessman and said two words: "Purple pimpernel?"

"What?" Past Agent Hessman frowned.

"Never mind," Claire replied, pointing after the Chinese men. "They went that-a-way."

"Two Chinese men running away from security," Ben added.

"Right. Thanks."

"Oh," Claire added as Past Agent Hessman started to dart off, "in about seven years, please think of getting a new shirt."

Past Agent Hessman tossed Claire a puzzled look and then ran off in the direction Ben had indicated.

"You didn't need to use the code-word to figure out who he was, you know," Ben remarked. "Not after the makeup job you did."

"I know," Claire replied. "I just wanted to try it out. Now how's about we take Grandpa here out for a stroll in a quieter locale?"

"Say, around back of the Convention Center?" Ben asked.

"Perfect," Claire replied. "The bad guys always try to break in through the back."

"Wait, I caught part of that," Dr. Weiss said as he glanced up. "Why do I have to be Grandpa?"

"The cane," Ben stated.

"Ah, I see." Dr. Weiss lowered his eyes again. "You know, the intricacies of this temporal radiation detector are amazing. I'm more and more convinced that the Chinese had some help, but the question is from whom."

The three stuck to their leisurely stroll while chaos rolled through the crowds.

☾

THE ALIENS STEP IN

Sue and Polson broke off into separate tangents. They had to corner the Chinese time travelers before they made it back inside the convention center. Sue couldn't run with all the crowds in the way, but she did manage a hurried dash, pushing her way past one suited intellectual after another. A few objections and annoyed looks here and there, but nothing to stop her—until a familiar voice smacked her in the ears.

"Young woman, it is impolite under any circumstances to be running through a crowd, but to shove aside someone like me aside could very well end you up in deep trouble."

She looked up to see General Karlson facing her, alongside a younger-looking Dr. Weiss.

"Oh, uh sorry, General Karlson."

"You know me?"

"Well, uh . . . purple pimpernel?"

"What?"

"Never mind."

While the past versions of General Karlson and Dr. Weiss looked at each other, puzzling over the strange phrase, Sue dashed past them, determined to stop the two Chinese spies. The culprits had nearly reached the entrance of the Convention Center. She wouldn't reach them in time—not with the crowds in the way.

What *did* stop the Chinese was the sudden appearance of a large wall—a wall by the name of Lieutenant Polson.

The limping man bounced off of the large Navy Seal's frame, while the other bounced off Polson's fist. They tumbled backward and leaped to their feet, backing away from Polson and turned around to see Past Agent Hessman and his men coming at them. They spun around to see Sue standing in the crowd with a threatening grin and then picked the only direction remaining. They dashed up a short flight of stone steps leading to a walkway that circled around the building as an upper landing.

Sue saw their course, but also realized that said walkway went completely around the building and came out with another set of stairs at the far side of the front entrance. The walkway would give the Chinese time travelers an opportunity to skirt around most of their pursuers and find their way back into the convention center.

"Polson, with me," she shouted.

Sue sprinted toward the other side of the front entrance and up the far stairway, determined to meet the Chinese time travelers head-on before they could enter the building. Polson was only a leap or two behind her. They sprinted down the walkway along the building's length. As Sue leaned into a sharp left turn, she reached out and grabbed hold of a corner rail to take the corner without missing a step. The two desperate-looking Chinese spies were just coming around from the other side, heading toward them, followed by the sound of shouting men.

Past Agent Hessman and the security guards.

The spies paused when they saw Sue, glanced behind them at the shouting, and then looked at the ground below the walkway.

Sue looked down at the same time. Midway between her and the spies, a set of steps led down to an open, ground-level courtyard behind the convention center.

Everyone accelerated toward those steps.

Sue heard Polson's footsteps running behind her. The beat stopped. She glanced over her shoulder to see Lieutenant Polson pole vault over the waist-high walkway wall into a tree. He slid down its trunk into a planter.

As Sue approached the stairs, the tall Chinese spy aimed a pistol at her. A double gunshot rang through the air. Sue ducked, weaving to one side as a bullet whistled past her ear.

The tall Chinese spy lurched backwards clutching his shoulder. Blood pooled under his hand. Sue spun around to see Past Agent Hessman holding out a pistol.

"Stop right there," Past Agent Hessman called.

The two Chinese spies—including the one with the injured shoulder—followed Lieutenant Polson's action and leaped over the outer stone wall. Sue bolted down the stairs.

THE ALIENS STEP IN

The Chinese spies landed in a short strip of grassy landscaping, did a tuck and roll back up to their feet, and started running and limping once again. Polson zeroed in on them quickly. To their right was Sue. To their left there was no one but an old, white-haired homeless man.

They veered toward the homeless man.

The limping Chinese spy was dropped by a punch to the throat from the homeless man. The other Chinese spy continued on, desperate and confused. He suddenly dropped too, this time from a hard cane to his gut.

The limping man rolled around, gurgling, and glanced up to see Agent Hessman disguised with makeup and an inside-out suit. Ben handed the cane that had felled the other spy back to Dr. Weiss.

"Sorry, but there was no time to ask," Ben told his friend.

"Huh? Oh, of course." Dr. Weiss studied the Chinese temporal radiation detector, oblivious to what had happened. "This is definitely a hidden function that I'm sure the Chinese didn't even know about, but as to what it does..."

☾

Up on the landing, Past Agent Hessman had his gun out, his security men flanking him, as he quickly surveyed the situation. An old man had dropped one of the Chinese spies, three tourists had felled the other, while a Black woman and a Navy Seal ran over to join the old man.

Past Agent Hessman did the one thing that Agent Hessman of any time would do. "Okay, every hold it right there. I don't know what's going on here, but I'm going to—"

Suddenly, the device in Dr. Weiss's hand emitted a high-pitched whine.

"That hidden function I mentioned," he said to Ben and Claire, "it just activated itself."

"Is that good or bad?" Claire asked.

"According to what this thing says," Dr. Weiss replied as he desperately consulted the device's small display, "it's putting out waves of temporal distortion."

"What?" Ben exclaimed. "But that's impossible!"

"Tell this thing that!" Dr. Weiss replied. "It's interacting with the background readings, but beyond that I have no idea what's happening."

The Chinese spy who was rolling at Ben's feet looked at the whining device in Dr. Weiss's hand, his eyes wide with fright. There was only one conclusion that anyone could make.

Both Agent Hessmans shouted, "Bomb!" and raised pistols. Time-traveling Agent Hessman aimed for the temporal radiation detector, Past Agent Hessman for the man holding it. Sue and Polson both hit the ground, and Claire clung to Ben like the frightened little girl she suddenly felt herself to be.

It ended not in an explosion but a brilliant flash of white light that encompassed them all. It was sourced not from the Chinese device but all around them.

CHAPTER TWELVE
THE INTERVENTION

AGENT HESSMAN AND HIS TEAM of time travelers suddenly found themselves back in their respective pods at the facility as the massive arms of the temporal chamber spun down, the wormhole collapsing with the abrupt end of their mission.

"What happened?" Agent Hessman demanded as a technician helped him out of his pod. "That flash of light was very unlike the normal return sequence."

"Unlike it at all," Dr. Weiss agreed as he staggered across the central platform.

Technicians helped the other time travelers from their pods, and General Karlson entered the chamber through the far-side door.

While Agent Hessman took off his jacket to pull it right-side out again, he noted that Sue stood alert and still battle-ready, as if unsure they had been returned to safety, even in the confines of the main Chamber. Claire clung to Ben uncertainly. Lieutenant Polson made a quick visual survey of the situation himself and stepped off the platform to join the general as soon as the technicians had freed him of the last set of wires.

"Sam." Ben turned to his friend. "You said that device has a hidden function. Did you do something with it?"

"I touched nothing," Dr. Weiss replied. "I was examining it when it self-activated. It started sending out"—he looked at his hands— "the device! Where is it?"

Agent Hessman frowned at Dr. Weiss's empty hands. "Is it possible the Chinese spies have it?" he asked.

"If the temporal radiation detector gets in the wrong hands . . ." Ben began.

"Any hands are the wrong hands for that thing," Dr. Weiss amended.

"Report!"

To the general's snapped command, everyone stopped chattering and joined the general and Polson.

Agent Hessman shook the talcum powder out of his hair and gave it a rough finger comb before pulling out a handkerchief to wipe the worst of the makeup off from his face. "We were in a confrontation, General," he stated. "Ourselves, the remainder of the Chinese team, and myself from the past and accompanying security team."

"I assume you succeeded in your mission?" the general asked.

"We never finished it, sir. We'd found this strange device the Chinese team was using—a temporal radiation detector—and Dr. Weiss was examining it when something happened."

"An explosion of time is the best way to describe it," Dr. Weiss explained. "The device seemed to be generating it, but then—white light; everywhere."

"General," Sue cut in, "you shouldn't have brought us back yet. The mission is not completed. Not by a long shot."

"So, you never got around to fixing things," the general asked thoughtfully.

"No, sir," Agent Hessman replied.

"Then that makes things even more puzzling."

"What do you mean?" Dr. Weiss asked.

"I mean, that time seems to have fixed itself. Everything is back to the way it should be. The base outside is as it should be, and there is no sign of anything unusual that computers can find in the way of history as we know it. Also, we aren't the ones who brought you back."

"What?" chorused Agent Hessman, Dr. Weiss, Sue, and Ben. Claire looked suddenly less frightened and frowned thoughtfully.

"The equipment suddenly reversed itself," the general continued, "and yet we picked up nothing of your recall signals."

Mr. Thomas came in behind the general, and he wore as stern a glare as any they'd seen him display. "What the hell is going on here?" he snapped. "History is back to the way it should be, but the fact that we aren't responsible is at least as disturbing as everything else."

"Um, if I may . . ." Claire seemed unconcerned about Mr. Thomas's mood as she pointed toward the main platform. "Maybe *he* might have an answer?"

All heads turned to the central platform. Standing in the center was a figure unlike anything Agent Hessman had seen in his life. Human in general shape only, it stood about half a foot taller than Lieutenant Polson, with six-fingered hands, webbed toes, large black eyes, large-flanged ears, and a thick mop of hair on its head that looked like thin, translucent, yellow noodles. The strange hair was neatly trimmed to its ears. Whiskers sprung from its nose, and its domed head, a little larger than most humans, had a slight depression in the center of its forehead. The creature had bare feet but wore a golden jumpsuit with a blue cape that came almost to its ankles.

It was also holding the Chinese temporal radiation detector in its hands—the one that Dr. Weiss had been examining—and it was making some adjustments to its controls.

"Be careful how you touch that!" Dr. Weiss cried reflexively.

"Sam," Ben said quickly, one hand to his shoulder, "somehow I think he knows a lot more about that thing than we do."

Lieutenant Polson stepped forward to the left of the small group, while Sue stepped forward to the right. The technicians who had been working

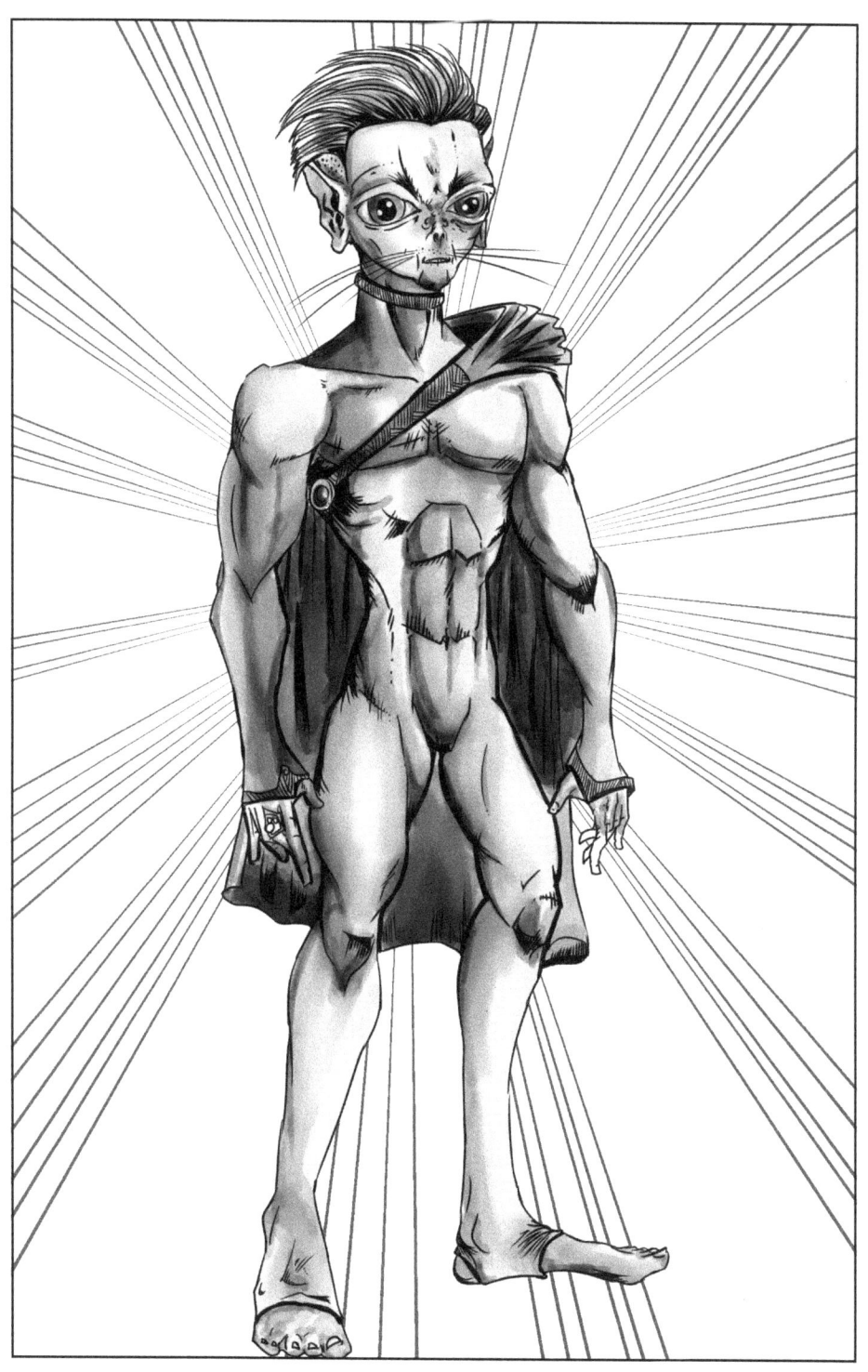

#2 – Sonsa Tabback – Alien Captain

on the equipment quickly backed off the platform, leaving it to the creature.

Everyone froze with fixed gazes upon the creature. Even Mr. Thomas held back as he narrowed his eyes suspiciously in its direction.

"Of course!" Dr. Weiss exclaimed as his eyes lit up with a fresh, boyish enthusiasm. "The odd coded signals we kept picking up in the temporal scanners. This is the source. This ... this ..."

"I am a Galnaran."

The creature spoke with a raspy voice as it looked up from its work. It held the Chinese device firmly in one hand, making no move to hand it over to anyone. Its face was nearly expressionless, as if looking over a room of naughty children with tired patience.

"Galnar," the creature continued, "is located in what you call Orion's Belt. My name is Sonsa Tabbak, and I am commander of the vessel currently in orbit around your world."

More silence, until the general stepped forward. At first Sue blocked his way with an arm and warning look, but he gently moved her arm out of the way. "It's okay, Agent Harris. I think it's quite evident that if he wants us dead, there is no way we could stop him."

With visible reluctance, Sue stepped to the side, and the general stepped forward to take his place at the head of the small assembly.

"I am General Karlson, commander of this base."

"But not currently the one in charge, if my information is correct," the alien stated.

Now it was Mr. Thomas who stepped forward, nothing but steely determination in his features.

"That would be me. I am Mr. Rutger Thomas, and I report directly to the president himself. You are the one who fixed up the timeline?"

"I am," the alien replied.

"The coded signals ..." Dr. Weiss began. "How long have your people been observing us?"

"Enough to know that you are Dr. Samuel Weiss, your companion is Professor Ben Stein, his mate is Mrs. Claire Hill-Stein ..."

"He remembered the hyphen," Claire whispered excitedly to Ben. "An alien remembered the hyphen."

". . . the leader of your missions is Special Agent Lou Hessman, and the bodyguard is Agent Sue Harris. The last two members of your team seem interchangeable, and I do not see Captain Robert Beck."

"He's under guard at the moment," the general answered. "So, your methods for observing us are far beyond our capability to detect or counter. What is it that you want of us?"

"I for one wouldn't mind a long chat with his scientists," Dr. Weiss said excitedly. "But first I think we should thank him. He did, after all, correct the mess that the Chinese spies made of history."

"I corrected the mess that *all* of you have made of your timeline," Sonsa Tabbak amended. He stepped forward a few paces, within arm's reach of the general. The action prompted Lieutenant Polson to reach for his gun—until Mr. Thomas snapped him a look.

"Lieutenant, what were you planning on doing?" Mr. Thomas demanded. "The creature just said that he has a vessel in orbit that can no doubt vaporize this entire base, and it appeared in our midst without the benefit of going through any doors. The best you can do is create the world's first interstellar diplomatic incident, and I, for one, will shoot you myself before I let that happen. Am I clear?"

"Sir," the Lieutenant replied and eased back into a slightly less alert posture.

The alien gave a slight nod in Mr. Thomas's direction and continued. "My world is part of the Interstellar Unity. And while I am sure that Dr. Weiss has several questions, some of which will be answered in due time, it is vitally important that I speak with you."

"I'm listening," the general said.

The alien took a moment to take them all in, its beady eyes taking a swift examination of each person present. "We have been observing your primitive time traveling and noted the risks these activities pose to yourselves."

"Exactly the reason for the mission," Lou stated. "The Chinese agents altered our history."

"The attempt at self-correction is noted, but you still fail to see the entire picture. Disruptions to your own time-space create waves that radiate out from your world to others nearby. You have failed to consider such disruptions and have no idea the impact they can have. Furthermore, a collapse of your own timeline, such as nearly happened, and the resultant explosion would have had catastrophic impacts on many other stars, beyond your means to conceive."

"Sam?" General Karlson immediately asked in aside.

"It's possible," the physicist replied with a slight nod. "We're really in the infancy of this science, but temporal distortion waves seem related to gravity waves, so it makes sense that anything affecting them would ripple along any interacting gravitational fields to nearby star systems. There's no telling how many other star systems our near disaster might have affected."

"*Inhabited* star systems," Sonsa Tabbak added. "While we have reversed the current changes to your timeline and stabilized the impending chrononic explosion, we still need to talk."

"I can have a conference room ready in five minutes," the general offered.

But the alien simply shook its head.

"I mean, we need to talk to *all* of you."

Before the general could inquire any further, Claire made a frightening deduction. "Uh, General? I think he means all of us humans. The planet as a whole."

To which the alien replied with a slow, single nod.

CHAPTER THIRTEEN
UNEXPECTED VISITOR

"IF I MAY," AGENT HESSMAN interjected, "a small question that my position as head of this base's security demands I ask."

"You wish to know how I got past all of your security, including your temporal neutral field, and everything else without being noticed," Sonsa Tabbak said.

"Not meaning to be rude, you understand," Agent Hessman added.

Sonsa Tabbak replied with a slight incline of his head. "A simple matter, really, when you consider how much more advanced my people are than yours. Cloaking technology, the ability to teleport, and the fact that your temporal technology is really in its infancy. Shall I go on?"

"No, that answer quite satisfies what I needed to ask. Please continue."

Sonsa Tabbak then returned his attention to the Chinese temporal radiation detector in his hand, turning it over once in his six-fingered hand with a thoughtful purse of his lips. "Hmm. I find it quite interesting the Chinese faction of your world appears to have developed something that is several centuries beyond them."

"That was my first thought," Dr. Weiss broke in. "What that device appears to do is well beyond anything I know of earth science."

"At any rate," the alien continued, "this bears further investigation."

Sonsa Tabbak pocketed the device within his jumpsuit and directed his gaze back at the group.

"My mission is to stop your world's dangerous activities before they hurt far more than your own history. To accomplish this, I will meet with a few certain of your leaders directing the time travel programs. Leaders from your own country, Russia, and China."

Agent Hessman casually reached into the pocket where he kept his secure cell phone, exposed it just enough to eye some of the icons on the screen, then thumbed one shaped like a small microphone.

"As head of this base and the American program," General Karlson spoke up, "I must then be one of those attending."

"And as head of your security," Agent Hessman said, "I must go with you."

Before the general could acknowledge Agent Hessman, Mr. Thomas spoke up, his tone stern. "I am the eyes and ears of the president himself! I must be present at that meeting."

"All quite agreeable," Sonsa Tabbak replied. "Special Agent Hessman, you can even take that small recording device you are trying to hide in your pocket."

Agent Hessman stopped, pulled his hand out of his pocket, and shrugged.

Sonsa Tabbak gestured in the direction of the chamber's exit and spoke again. "You have access to your world's sensor grid within your main control room, I believe. If you would kindly direct those resources to a position one thousand miles directly above this base, you will see my vessel. It has been hidden from your view all this time but has now been ordered to make itself known."

"How in the hell could we not be aware of a spaceship in the sky above this sensitive facility?" Mr. Thomas asked.

Sonsa Tabbak replied, "We have the ability to prevent your observation of whatever we choose."

"See to it," the general ordered a technician. "I want every satellite, telescope, and ground-based radar dish available aimed at that position and the results up on the main screen by the time we get to the control room."

The technician hurried off with a rapid nod while the general turned a more polite tone to the alien. "If you will allow me to play host and escort you to the control room."

Sonsa Tabbak replied with another incline of his head. The general led the way out, with Agent Hessman and the others right behind him.

Their walk through the base was not long. Troops and technicians snapped to attention on either side of the hall wherever they went as curious eyes regarded the singular alien presence in their midst. It was not short enough a walk, however, to prevent one person from throwing caution to the wind and stepping up beside the alien for a quick word or two.

Specifically, Claire.

"So, what can you tell me about your people and your world?" she asked. "So many questions I don't really know where to begin."

"I am sure that you will find a good angle," Sonsa Tabbak told her. "You are a very good reporter. And storyteller."

"You know of me and my work?" Claire asked, delighted.

"Some of our best information on your cross-temporal travels comes from your reports. We find them most... amusing."

"Amusing," she beamed. "That's good, right?" She then stepped back and turned to Ben. "Amusing is good, right? I mean, they are aliens quite a lot more advanced than us, so I wouldn't expect them to be shocked or anything."

He shrugged. "Considering that we know nothing about these beings—other than what we've heard the last five minutes—about five more minutes of you questioning him, and you'll be the world's foremost expert on them."

"Me, a foremost?" she said, a smile brightening her face.

As they turned down a branching hall with the control center directly ahead, Claire stepped back up to Sonsa Tabbak with a barrage of questions.

"So, tell me something about your planet and its people. Are there other types of aliens there, or just your specific kind? How many alien civilizations have you encountered out there? Why don't you wear shoes? Is it because the ground is so smooth on your world that you don't have to worry about stepping on anything? And you're a male, right? Do you have any children?"

The reply was a chuckle from the alien just as the doors swung open before them. "Miss Hill-Stein, you are as determined an individual as reports have made you out to be."

The screens of the control room were already filled with fresh images by the time the group walked in. Several smaller screens of varying quality displayed the same radar image: a small blip. The central main screen showed the sharpest image: that of a large vessel suspended against the backdrop of stars with the earth below it.

At the sight of the general and his party marching in, the senior technician, Jason, jumped to his feet, snapped off a quick salute, and made his report.

"Sir, data coming in now, but there is indeed a vessel where none had been before. The main screen's image is coming from one satellite that was sitting no more than sixty miles away from it in the same orbit, but it never captured a thing until five minutes ago."

The general stopped midway to his command dais, regarding the image, while Dr. Weiss went over to the nearest free terminal to type in some commands. Agent Hessman studied some of the text readouts along the edges of the side screens.

"What am I looking at?" General Karlson snapped. "Give me some scale on this thing."

"General," Dr. Weiss called back from his terminal, "from what I can tell, that vessel is five miles long."

"Did you say *miles?*" Ben asked, shock registering on his face.

"Confirmed, sir," Jason replied. "We can still get only the most general

#3 – Galnaran Space Ship

of profiles, but the alien vessel measures approximately five miles across. Spectroscopics can give no indication of the hull's composition, and radar cannot penetrate the interior."

"That is all your level of technology will be able to ascertain," Sonsa Tabbak stated. "Do I, as you would say, have your attention now?"

A small sea of stunned looks and quietly nodding heads was the reply.

"You do," the general quietly replied. "This meeting you want; when is it to be held?"

"Immediately."

A flicker of light and a snap of ozone, and Sonsa Tabbak was gone . . . along with General Karlson, Special Agent Hessman, and Mr. Thomas, leaving everyone else shocked and scrambling.

CHAPTER FOURTEEN
TOUR OF FORCE

THEY MATERIALIZED IN A HIGH-CEILINGED, circular room with red walls and dark brown carpeting. Agent Hessman rubbed his shoe over it. It looked and felt more like natural grass growing straight from the floor than a carpet.

Light came from a large circular ceiling fixture and provided enough illumination to qualify as summer midday in Arizona. The only exit from the chamber seemed to be an open archway that led to a tunnel-shaped corridor.

Agent Hessman studied the room. General Karlson and Mr. Thomas were present, but so were three Chinese representatives and three others that Agent Hessman guessed to be Russian. Two aliens who looked like Sonsa Tabbak, but about a foot shorter, were also present.

The humans appeared to be in shock. One of the Russians spoke in a tone that sounded midway between shock and anger. The Chinese spoke in quiet whispers.

Sonsa Tabbak took his position at the front of the room and waited a few moments before speaking. "As I said, our meeting is to be held immediately, and the tour I shall now lead you on is for everyone's benefit. Furthermore, what you are about to witness is simultaneously being transmitted to all of your respective governmental rulers. Now if you will just follow me..."

"He could have at least waited for me to finish getting off the clown makeup," Agent Hessman grumbled, rubbing at his face with his handkerchief.

Sonsa Tabbak started to lead the way across the room to the one portal, but one of the Russians immediately voiced an objection.

"You will tell us now where you are taking us to. That archway could lead us to our slaughter."

"Or some sort of alien mind control," one of the Chinese contingent stated.

"I admit to a few questions myself," Mr. Thomas agreed, though more quietly. "Agent Hessman, your assessment."

Agent Hessman stepped forward to aim a critical eye at the curved doorway, noticing Sonsa Tabbak watching him curiously. The hallway it opened up to was similarly curved and lit with a dim red light, the walls crisscrossing with intersecting lines of a darker color. He only needed to give it a brief look before he stepped more confidently towards it. "Don't you people recognize an airport scanner when you see one?"

"Essentially correct," Sonsa Tabbak stated. "The scanner tunnel will examine you all for weapons and pathogens. If any pathogens are detected, you will be sprayed with a disinfectant. Any weapons detected will be confiscated and returned later. Special Agent Hessman, perhaps you would like to be the first. Simply walk through to the other end. I will follow after all of you have gone through."

With a nod, Agent Hessman walked up to the portal and paused to straighten his suit. On the side of the archway, a panel slid open, exposing a chute. Agent Hessman took the hint. He pulled out his gun, dropped it into the chute, and stepped into the tunnel.

He walked at a steady pace. A series of laser beams kept in step with him. He felt nothing, but he was quite certain that every measure of him was being scanned and recorded. When he reached the end, a fine mist sprayed out over him, and then he stepped out into a more brightly lit chamber.

"Like walking through a carwash, complete with the wax spray at the end," he remarked.

Next to come through was the general, followed by Mr. Thomas, the latter depositing two guns into the chute. The Russians objected the most, with one of them dropping two guns into the chute only after a bit of arguing with Sonsa Tabbak. Midway down the tunnel, the same man was stopped by a shimmering force field as a chute rose up from the floor. After he dropped a third gun into it, the chute and force field withdrew, allowing him to continue.

Only when all the Russians and Chinese were through did Sonsa Tabbak himself take the walk, joining them in the room beyond.

It was more of a waiting room, plain but for the outline of what Agent Hessman guessed to be an automatic sliding door that remained closed. When Sonsa Tabbak made his way across the room, he raised his right hand. A strange ring on his second finger briefly glimmered, and the door slid open before him.

Then he turned to face his guests. "What you are about to see is what we term an exploratory class vessel. It carries everything we need while away from civilized space, including power, manufacturing facilities, portable wormhole generator, and so on. Please do not touch anything unless I tell you as it could be dangerous if handled wrongly."

At these words, Agent Hessman glanced over to the Chinese with a few words for their ears.

"Hear that? No trying to steal anyone's technology again."

One of the Chinese representatives shrugged as if he didn't know what Agent Hessman was talking about, but Agent Hessman knew better. He would keep an eye on both them and the Russians through the remainder of this trip.

THE ALIENS STEP IN

They went through the mysterious door into an intersection of corridors, all a brightly lit pale bluish white, with walls that felt like soft plastic to the touch. Five different halls fanned out before them, each bustling with more aliens like Sonsa Tabbak.

"Please do not stray," Sonsa Tabbak announced, leading them down the second hall from the left.

Agent Hessman did a quick double-check to see if the phone in his pocket was recording everything being said, then cast a swift eye for the others. He noticed one member of the Chinese contingent falling back, his eyes darting between the other corridors. Just as he stepped toward the one on the right, Agent Hessman gripped the man's shoulder. "Try to stay with the tour group," Agent Hessman said with a false smile, "or I might be forced to feed your privates parts to one of the Russians."

"Stupid Americans," the other spat, "you have no idea—"

"I heard that," Agent Hessman said as he removed his hand. "Now come along."

"You heard. Then you speak Chinese?"

"Of course not." It took Agent Hessman a moment to realize the importance of what they had both just said. It took the other man a moment longer.

Agent Hessman eyed Sonsa Tabbak suspiciously and hurried to the front of the group.

"The first sight," Sonsa Tabbak relayed, "will be of one of our manufacturing facilities."

"Your mouth," Agent Hessman carefully noted. "Just now, it wasn't moving when you spoke. And I understood the words of the Chinese representatives when I don't speak Chinese."

"Observant," Sonsa Tabbak replied. "Simple telepathy. Nothing remarkable. I use it to communicate now with all of you so that my meaning will be clear in your native languages, and I set up a similar field around me that allows you to understand one another as well. A simple measure to foster proper communication."

#4 – Dicta-Ring (Illustration by Joshua Smith)

"Is that what the ring is for?"

It was the general who now spoke, indicating the strange ring on the second finger of the alien's right six-fingered hand. It was made of metal in the shape of a pentagon, with three different three-dimensional cones projecting up from it: one red, another yellow, and the third an iridescent blue.

"This," Sonsa Tabbak said, briefly bringing up his hand, "is merely my Dicta-Ring. It enables me to authenticate items. It's similar to the wax seal on one of your documents but more complex. It encodes objects on the atomic level and is also used as a security pass for certain areas of this vessel. Before anyone thinks of stealing it, however, note that each ring is telepathically attuned to its wearer. Now, if you will kindly note the left-hand wall."

Sonsa Tabbak brought them to a stop and placed his right hand flat against the wall. The stones on the ring flashed in a quick combination of colors. Then, twenty feet to either side of them, the wall suddenly faded into transparency, giving them all a view of what lay beyond.

Everyone was struck silent. Mr. Thomas carefully eyed every detail while Agent Hessman discreetly removed his cell phone from his pocket to record the view.

A small, mechanized valley lay below them, stretching well over a thousand feet in any given direction. The valley was filled with towering machines that looked as though they could stamp out a full-sized tank in a single go. Other structures that appeared to be hundred-foot-tall Tesla coils powered some alien machine that produced a line of unfathomable devices on a rolling assembly line. There were cranes large enough to pick up and haul a full-sized fishing boat across the vast chamber. In one far section, Agent Hessman saw a line of hundred-foot-tall cylinders twenty feet wide, tubes from the tops of each to pumping something out into other pieces of equipment. There were pipes a dozen feet across, lasers swiftly carving designs into ten-foot-thick blocks of metal, and machines with a score of robotic arms all converging onto a given apparatus.

All of this was contained by a single chamber held within the massive vessel orbiting the Earth.

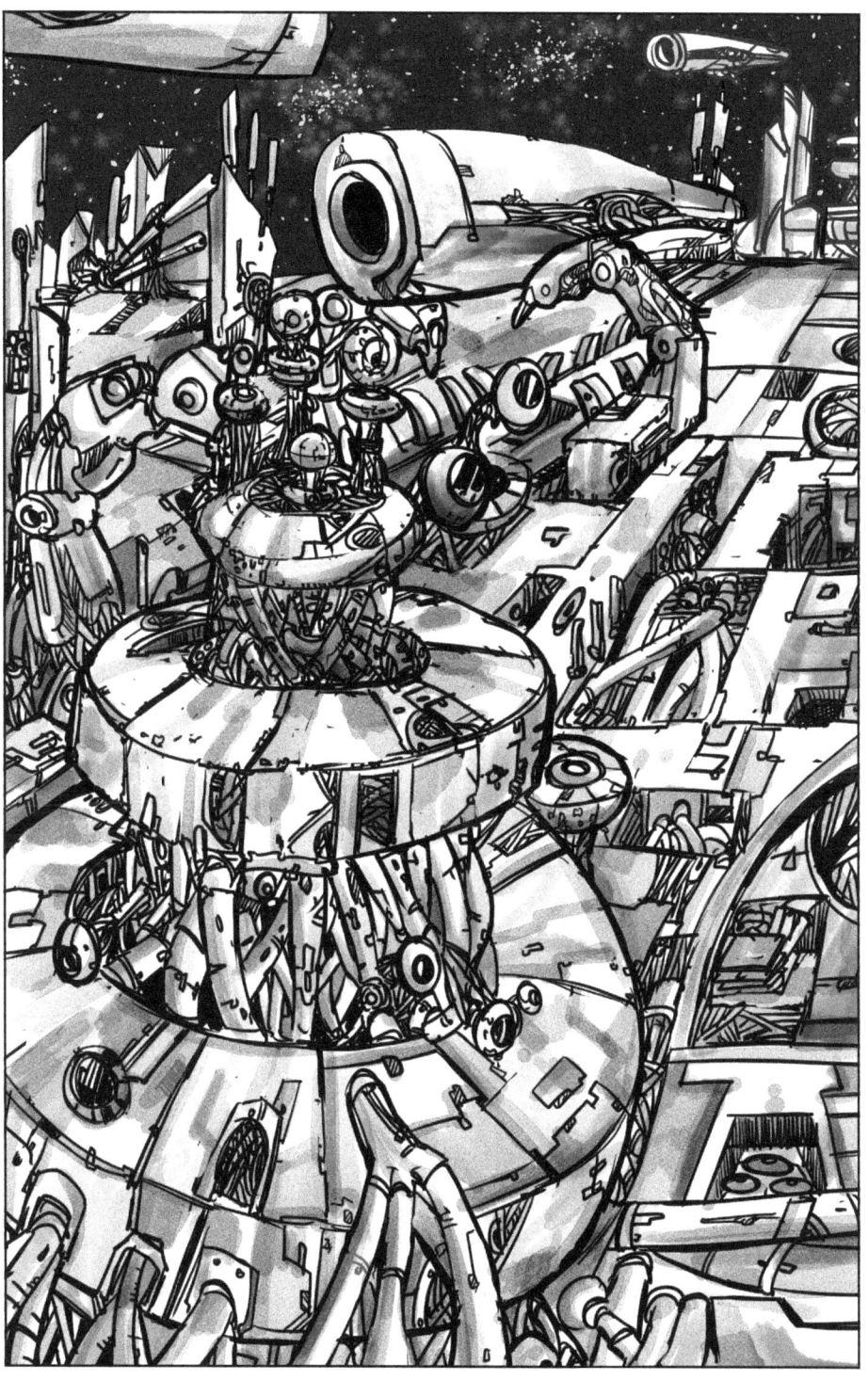

THE ALIENS STEP IN

Sonsa Tabbak waited a few moments before again touching his hand to the wall, rendering it opaque once more.

"Just a sample," Sonsa Tabbak explained. "Now if you will all kindly stand in the center of the hall, we can continue on to the next exhibit. It's only a mile down this same hall."

"Mile sounds like lots of walking for weak Americans," one of the Russians stated with a grin. "Perhaps should order out taxi."

The grin, however, was quickly erased as they discovered the floor beneath them was moving and carrying them along with it—but only the sections of floor they stood upon. Other aliens walking that same hall moved at their own paces, chatting amongst themselves, while the squares of flooring beneath the humans zipped along, dodging around aliens as needed.

A Chinese representative grabbed onto one of his companions in brief shock, while even the boldly speaking Russian was caught off guard.

They were moving fast, but as Agent Hessman noted, it didn't feel like they were moving.

"What you would call 'engineering' is up ahead," Sonsa Tabbak calmly stated. "This vessel draws its power from what you would term a 'white hole.' The white hole itself is comparatively small, but the shielding needed to contain it is, by necessity, quite large. Ah, here we are."

Their movement slowed as they rounded a corner, concluding in what appeared to be a dead-end alcove. As they came to a stop, though, Sonsa Tabbak again pressed his ring hand against the wall, and the alcove revealed itself to be a balcony overlooking another vast facility.

This time there was but one single object. It was surrounded by control panels and support equipment manned by aliens and some robotic assistants. To Agent Hessman, the object appeared to be about the size of a nuclear power containment vessel: a large metal sphere three hundred feet across that took up the entire far end of the chamber. It seemed to glow from within.

"The containment walls are a hundred feet thick and composed of a material you have yet to discover," Sonsa Tabbak explained. "They include

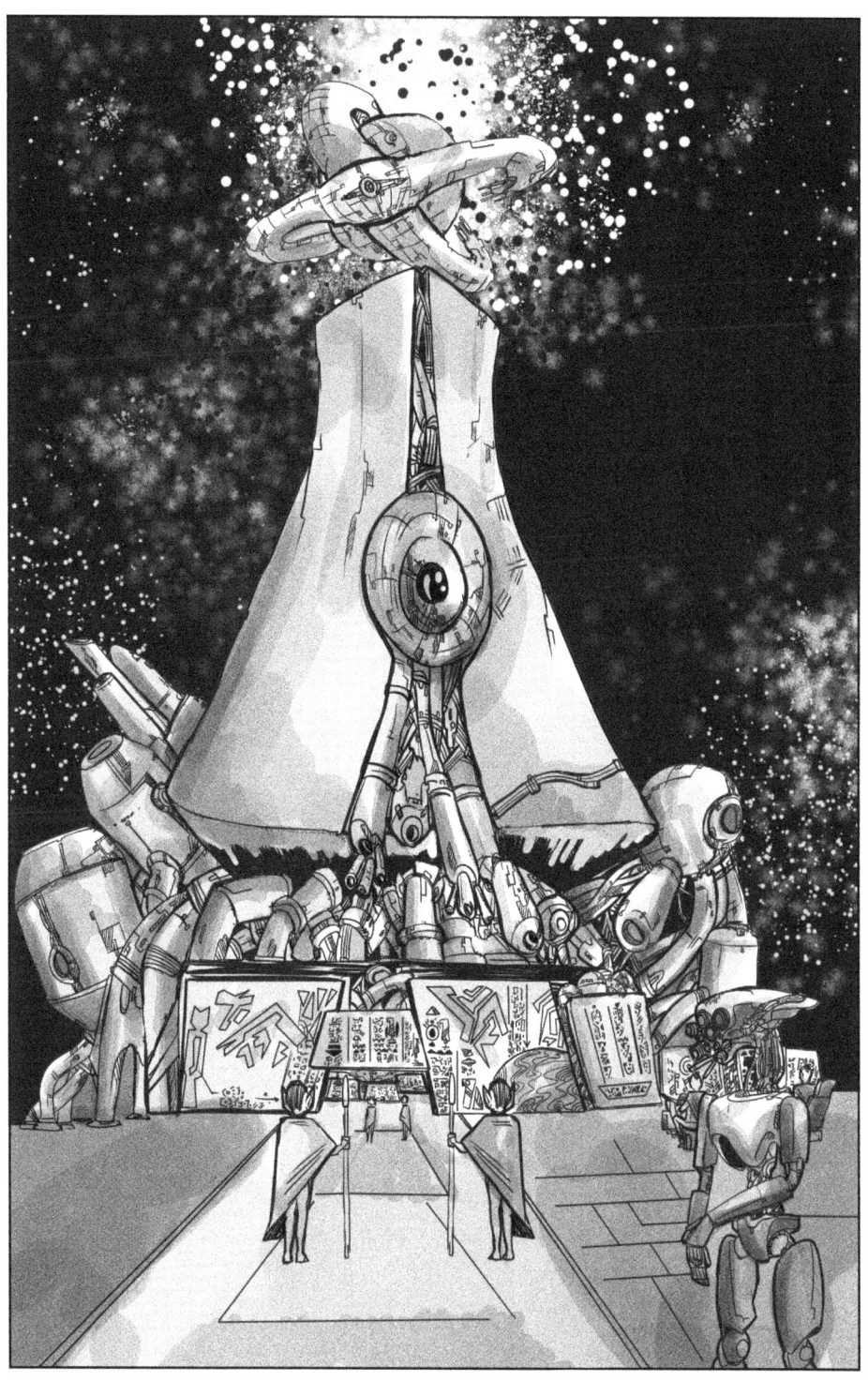

multiple layers of force fields. The glow you see is the residual radiation that still manages to get through, but it is well within spec and harmless."

"A hundred feet thick and still glowing is not what I would call harmless," one of the Russians remarked.

"Rest assured," Sonsa Tabbak stated, "the white hole generator is quite secure."

Hand to wall, glow of ring, and the wall was solid once more.

"Our next stop is the bridge where you will witness the required demonstration of power."

"You mean there's more?" the general asked.

"Of course," Mr. Thomas said with a knowing nod. "This is all just the support equipment. They would dare not show us anything really dangerous."

The sections of flooring beneath their feet once again began to move, carrying them down another long, brightly lit hall.

One of the Chinese shielded his eyes. "Why do you keep the halls so brightly lit? Half this light would seem more than sufficient."

"Brightly lit?" For a moment, Sonsa Tabbak looked puzzled until revelation lit up on his face. "Ah yes, you do not know. My world has two suns, so we are used to this as our normal ambient lighting. We have no night as your world does. I am sorry if this gives you discomfort, but it should still be within the parameters of what you can physically tolerate."

The moving sections of the floor finally stopped before an arched doorway. This time Sonsa Tabbak used his ring to slide the door panel aside and allow them to walk through. "This is the bridge," he announced.

The bridge was a large circular chamber, its perimeter sporting what Agent Hessman assumed to be regularly spaced control stations. Each station had an alien standing before it, a flat panel of popup holographic controls, and a hovering holographic display screen. There was nothing that might be termed a main screen, and the center of the room was empty of any furnishings or devices. In its entirety, the bridge looked to be about a hundred and fifty feet across.

THE ALIENS STEP IN

"If you will all step into the center," Sonsa Tabbak directed, "then you can view what I have to show you on the main screen."

"I see no screen," the noisy Russian remarked.

"Simply gather in the middle of the room. Then you will see," Sonsa Tabbak said.

They did as they were told, and Agent Hessman took in as much of his surroundings as he could in a few quick glances.

Once they were all in a circle around Sonsa Tabbak, the alien raised his right hand and the ring on it started to glow.

What the ring activated this time was, in a word, astounding.

It seemed as though they were floating upon the sky, looking down at the terrain far below. Every detail indicated they might actually be floating outside the spaceship. It was convincing enough to startle the Chinese, who groped about for something to grab onto, but it only took Agent Hessman a moment to realize the truth of it. The ring of manned control stations hovered along with them.

"No breeze and still the same temperature," he noted. "We're still on the bridge. This would seem to be a very good holographic projection."

"Our standard interface," Sonsa Tabbak explained. "Now, if you will look below."

Agent Hessman looked down to see an abandoned western ghost town in the middle of the American Desert. No one and nothing else around for miles.

"Our equipment confirms there is little more than a prairie dog around for many miles," Sonsa Tabbak said.

The way he said it sent a chill down Agent Hessman's spine, and he braced himself for what might happen next. Sonsa Tabbak spoke a few words in his own strange language. One moment, the ghost town was there, the next, it simply was not. The buildings turned into a faint outline of dust that dropped to the ground. Even the noisy Russian fell silent. The view held for a moment before it switched off, and they were once again standing in the open center of the bridge.

"Okay," a solemn General Karlson admitted. "You've made your point."

"Have I?" Sonsa Tabbak replied, his gaze taking in all three groups. "Normally, we would not interfere with your development; however your experimentation with something as dangerous as time travel makes this necessary. That, and this." He took the Chinese temporal radiation detector from his pocket and held it up for all to see.

"The technology displayed by this device demands our presence be revealed. So, I will ask"— he faced the Chinese group— "from where you got this technology?"

Agent Hessman kept a careful eye on the Chinese delegation and the expression on Sonsa Tabbak's face. He felt Mr. Thomas's eyes closely focused on him.

"You have no legal authority over us," one of the Chinese men replied.

"We are a sovereign nation subject to our own laws and no one else's," another stated in a firm voice.

"I am here to neither represent any presumed legal authority nor quibble with your own," Sonsa Tabbak stated. "If it comes to it, I will vaporize your entire scientific and industrial complex rather than risk your continued use of this technology. Now, where did this device come from? How did you know to manufacture it?"

They exchanged looks for a moment before one of the Chinese contingent reluctantly spoke up.

"One of our scientists designed it. That is the truth and all we know."

"Hmm," Sonsa Tabbak mused, "I can see you at least believe that to be true. I do, however, have my doubts."

The alien regarded them for a moment longer before he put the temporal radiation detector back into his jumpsuit. Then he addressed everyone. "There will be a further meeting scheduled, one involving a trip to my home world. This will be a diplomatic mission with representatives from the United States, Russia, and China. You will be given a few days to select your teams and prepare accordingly."

"And the purpose of this diplomatic mission?" Mr. Thomas asked.

"To discuss the future," Sonsa Tabbak replied, "as well as a possible gift."

A gift? Agent Hessman wondered. That one word had everyone exchanging looks within their respective groups: some eagerly, others with deep suspicion.

"Three days," Sonsa Tabbak said. "This meeting is now at an end."

The bridge vanished around them.

CHAPTER FIFTEEN
RETURN

SUDDENLY, AGENT HESSMAN APPEARED BACK in the middle of the base control room with General Karlson and Mr. Thomas. A flurry of anxious activity came to a screeching halt at their sudden reappearance.

Sue snapped out a salute to the general. "Sir! We've searched the entire base on the off chance that you and the alien had gone somewhere we could actually get to."

"We've been on the alien ship," General Karlson replied. "We had a rather eye-opening experience. Hessman, your assessment."

"I agree with the alien," Agent Hessman replied. "The Chinese told the truth that one of their scientists created that temporal radiation detector. Or at least, that's the truth that he knows."

"But the alien has his doubts," Mr. Thomas added. "Yes, I saw that too. Agent Hessman, I assume you were recording everything being said?"

Agent Hessman pulled out his phone and held it up. "Every alien word they said and whatever background chatter we heard in the halls."

"Do you mind if I have a look at that? I'd like to do some analysis."

Heads turned toward the voice. It was Samantha, on her feet but still in her hospital gown, with Claire supporting her on one side and a nurse on the other standing in the control room doorway.

Samantha offered a weak smile as Dr. Weiss rushed over to her side.

"My dear, you should not be on your feet like this," he said.

"I'm fine," she replied. "I just needed a little walk around."

She carefully hugged Dr. Weiss, then turned a smiling face in Agent Hessman's direction.

"Lou, I wanted to thank you. I've no doubt if not for you I wouldn't be walking around right now . . . or thinking."

Agent Hessman nodded curtly and handed his phone to her. "Analyzing this should give you something to do quietly as you're recovering. You need your rest."

Agent Hessman quickly turned to the general. He glanced back at Samantha and was saddened by the puzzled look on her face. He wished he had sounded more concerned, but that wasn't his way.

"First things first," General Karlson commanded. "I want Cassidy and that black op team of his packed up and out of here within the hour."

"Amend that," Mr. Thomas broke in. "They are to be sent out for trial and debriefing. I also want all of their stolen future tech rounded up and secured. No one's to so much as think about what any of it might do."

"We have a problem with that," Sue reported. "It's all disappeared."

Agent Hessman's ears perked up.

"Disappeared?" the general asked. "Explain."

"Vanished," Sue elaborated. "Not a single box left. I even traced where some of it was shipped to and contacted those locations. They've also lost track of it."

"We suspect it was the aliens' doing," Ben said. "Just as well too, I suppose."

"No doubt," General Karlson agreed. "Okay, this is what I want to see. Agent Hessman, get a team sent out to that ghost town to collect any available data on how it was destroyed, what's left of it, everything."

Agent Hessman nodded.

"Dr. Weiss, I need you to come up with some theories about how the aliens got through our defenses, how they transported us, everything. Lou, you, me, and Mr. Thomas here should also each write down our perspectives on what we experienced while it's still fresh in our minds."

Agent Hessman nodded again and reached for his phone.

"Agreed," Mr. Thomas snapped.

"Lou, I also need a team for that diplomatic mission to the alien planet. The alien also mentioned a possible gift. I want some speculation about what that could be."

Agent Hessman busily punched numbers into his phone.

"Gifts from such an advanced culture?" Dr. Weiss immediately beamed. "That could be anything from a cultural exchange to some advanced alien technology."

"Write that up in a report," the general snapped. "That and all reports are due in twenty-four hours. Come on everyone, hop to it!"

While the control room turned into a beehive of activity, Agent Hessman stole another glance at Samantha. She still looked puzzled or maybe sad. As soon as her gaze turned his way, he quickly looked at his feet. Lou had to use all the discipline he could muster to contain his growing feelings for Samantha. It was like a battle of the titans within Lou as his "nothing but business" attitude battled his personal feelings.

"You look tired, Samantha," Claire said. "Let's go back to your room."

She and the nurse escorted Samantha away still clutching Agent Hessman's recorder to her chest.

CHAPTER SIXTEEN
DEBRIEFING

THE NEXT MORNING, GENERAL KARLSON called everyone to the base conference room. Agent Hessman—now cleaned up from his makeup job—Dr. Weiss, Sue, Ben and Claire, Mr. Thomas, and Samantha, who was seated in a wheelchair, promptly responded. The mood was as uneasy as the expression on Mr. Thomas's face was strict and cold. Samantha spared a sidelong glance to Agent Hessman as she rolled up to her place at the table. Agent Hessman paid attention only to the general.

"Sam," the general began, "what did you find?"

Dr. Weiss brought out a jar of darkly colored dirt that he placed on the conference table and slid it slightly forward. "We retrieved a few canisters of dust from the ghost town site and some control samples from the soil of a region immediately adjacent. The ghost town samples have a high degree of carbon compared to the control samples, which tells me that the buildings were reduced to their constituent molecular components. Completely broken down."

"And just how would that have been accomplished?" the general asked.

"A... disintegration ray of some sort?" Dr. Weiss said with an exaggerated shrug. "I really don't know."

"Can you make an educated guess?" the general pressed.

"At this point, a few comic books suggest better explanations than anything I can come up with. In a mere moment, with not so much as any residual radiation that we can detect, no flash or anything, those old buildings simply fell apart."

"I see." The general pursed his lips thoughtfully for a moment. "How did the alien Sonsa Tabbak get inside this base despite shielding, our underground location, and any number of precautions on our part?"

Dr. Weiss again shrugged. "Well, if you want, I can toss around terms like 'quantum tunneling' and 'entanglement' to make you feel like I have an inkling of how he did it, but that would be pure suppositional bluffing."

"What about how they transported us up to their ship like that?" the general pressed.

"Refer to my previous answer," Dr. Weiss replied.

"Sam, were you able to determine *anything*?"

"General, the truth is that we really have no idea how they did what they did. Their science is beyond anything I've yet conceived."

General Karlson scowled. "Given all the money and effort we have committed to science, why do we seem to have such an inadequate understanding of—"

"Bottom-line it for me, Dr. Weiss. Does this mean that we are defenseless against these aliens?" Mr. Thomas said abruptly.

Dr. Weiss scanned the circle of concerned faces. "Completely, sir," was his answer.

"I have never felt so vulnerable," General Karlson blurted.

Silence reigned for a moment as Samantha produced the cell phone Agent Hessman had given her. "I would add that if the aliens knew Lou was recording them, they could have stopped him, yet they did not. They allowed him to record everything. Conclusion? The aliens know they have nothing to fear from any of us or our world."

"And what of the recording itself?" General Karlson asked.

"My team was unable to make anything out of it," she replied. "We simply do not have enough samples of their speech to create a language base. According to your reports, most of their communication was done telepathically, and that's not something this phone or anything we possess can record. I'm sorry."

She slid the phone across the table toward Agent Hessman, trying to catch his eye in the process. But his gaze barely touched upon hers as he swept the phone up from the table and back into his pocket. His attention never deviated from the discussion.

Samantha frowned.

"Samantha," Claire said, "I was wondering if you could get me—"

Samantha reached into a pocket of her hospital gown and produced a small thumb drive.

"A copy for your archives?" she smiled at the reporter. "With the general's permission, of course."

"A backup copy is a good idea," the general agreed. "But please remember, Claire, that you are still under the usual nondisclosure agreements."

"Of course," Claire smiled. "I report stories that no one will ever read. Except, apparently, some aliens from a faraway world, and possibly mole men from the center of the earth for all we know."

The comment got a brief chuckle from Ben and a smirk from Sue.

Samantha slid the thumb drive across the table towards Claire, who then pocketed it.

"Frivolity aside," Mr. Thomas stated, "we need to know what those aliens are saying."

The general agreed. "Being able to understand the enemy's language is the first step to understanding how they will act."

"We don't know that they *are* an enemy," Ben pointed out. "They straightened out the temporal mess we were in, so that's a point in their favor."

"They aren't allies," Mr. Thomas countered. "They are basically complete strangers. That makes them at least a potential enemy until proven otherwise, Professor Stein."

"But how can you make such an assumption?" Ben countered.

"Because it's in my job description to protect this country from all enemies foreign and domestic," Mr. Thomas snapped back. "We know nothing about them so we must assume the worst until proven otherwise."

"It sounds like a horrible way to live," Claire stated quietly.

"It is the way it must be done if others such as yourself are to be allowed to live with illusions of a perfect, peaceful world," Mr. Thomas replied. "I protect the sheep from wolves that the flock is unaware of. Now, if you are finished playing Little Mary Sunshine, we have other items to discuss."

In response to Claire's hurt look, Ben wrapped an arm around her waist and pulled her a little closer. Across the table, Sue looked like she wanted to do something very hurtful to Mr. Thomas.

General Karlson held up a hand. "Regarding the matter of language," he said, "Sam, how long do you think it would be to find a way to intercept their communications and gather enough data to decode the alien language?"

Dr. Weiss sat back in his chair, lips pursed in thought. "As a conservative estimate, I would say centuries at the least. If they are using some sort of quantum encoding to encrypt their communications, it would take our current computers the lifetime of the universe to break. We would need to develop quantum computers ourselves, which could take at least fifty years for a practical first-generation model. Then if they're using multiple languages in their communications, or some sort of verbal code much like what the code talkers of the Second World War used—"

"Okay," the general cut him off. "I get the idea. It's impossible."

"Not technically," Dr. Weiss countered, "just extremely improbable."

"And within the time frame of a few days?" the general prompted.

"Oh yeah, that would be completely impossible," Dr. Weiss agreed.

"Then to sum up," General Karlson stated, "we are completely helpless before them." He allowed a few moments of silence to let that fact sink in.

After a couple of moments, the general spoke again. "We need to know more about what and who we're dealing with. They want us to send up a team for this meeting of theirs, so we'll just have to make sure it consists of people who are well practiced in sniffing out information. Lou, the team will consist of yourself, Sue, Ben, Claire, and Sam."

"And me," Mr. Thomas insisted. "As the President's direct representative—"

"And Mr. Thomas," General Karlson agreed. "You will all go to wherever it is these aliens take you, find out as much as you can about them, what they want, and anything else that piques your interest."

"General," Agent Hessman said, "from what I could see, that alien, Sonsa Tabbak, is investigating something of his own. I saw suspicion in his eyes."

"Then you can also look into figuring out what the *aliens* are investigating as well," the general replied. "We're in the middle of something, and I want to know what it is."

"General, if I may," Claire spoke up, "what about Captain Beck?"

The general let out a heavy sigh and shook his head once before answering. "He is still being questioned to determine if his admittance of the Chinese doctor had anything to do with the sudden gaining of time travel technology by the Chinese. I know you like him, and you're about to argue how he only had everyone's best interest in mind, but that was a major security breach. Also, very probably treason."

"I understand," Claire said with a dejected sigh.

"General," Samantha raised her hand, "I'd like to volunteer to go along as well. I may be of some help figuring out the alien technology."

Agent Hessman turned briefly in her direction and spoke with cool formality. "Miss Weiss, you can barely stand. This mission is too dangerous, and you're still recovering."

Samantha's eyes fell to the table.

"He's right," the general agreed. "I'm afraid you'll have to sit this one out, Sam."

Samantha looked up again, her eyes on Agent Hessman. Hurt, lonely eyes.

"If that is all," the general announced, "this meeting is at an end. Lou, get your team ready with everything you think might be needed for your little trip. Dismissed."

Agent Hessman was the first one on his feet and out the door, his back turned to Samantha.

CHAPTER SEVENTEEN
PERSONAL FEELINGS

AGENT HESSMAN WAS SETTING A swift pace down the hall when he heard a call behind him.

"Lou, wait up."

It was Samantha's voice, the sound of her wheelchair nearing as fast as its motorized wheels could move. Agent Hessman paused in his tracks but did not look back. The scent of gardenias swept over him. When Samantha rolled to a stop by his side, he did not look down at her.

"Lou, why are you being so distant? I don't know whether to kiss you or slug you. You save my life and then call me 'Miss Weiss.' Really? What's going on with you? And *look* at me when I speak to you."

Agent Hessman fixed his gaze straight ahead down the hall. "Miss Weiss, this mission is very dangerous as it is. If I am to succeed, I cannot afford to have any... personal attachments... no matter what my feelings in the matter may or may not be."

"That's it, then," she realized aloud. "You're blaming yourself for what happened to me on that trip to the future. Lou, those future Russians made the first move in coming after me. *You* saved me. In fact, if it weren't for you, the mission they'd programmed me for might have gone off and then where would we be? You *saved* me."

"At the price of seeing your brain nearly blank-slated," he countered, his voice level.

"But I'm better now. Time corrected itself and here I am. Lou, I lo—"

"Please don't say it," Agent Hessman said sharply. "I must maintain my focus. My top priority is the security of this country, and to some degree, this world. There are hard decisions that I have to make. I can't afford to have that decision making process interrupted by other influences."

"Like me."

"Like you. Every decision I make runs the risk of endangering everyone on my team. But sometimes, it just has to be done. Suppose I hold back on such a decision for fear of loosing . . . someone, and the result is the downfall of this nation. Or worse."

"I . . . I suppose I understand," Samantha admitted. "I still think you're as wrong as a five-sided triangle, but I understand. You're so afraid of losing me that you won't even admit to yourself that you love me."

"I am a special agent in charge of the security of this project, Miss Weiss. I cannot afford the luxury of loving anyone."

"Ben and Claire make it work," she reminded him. "Quite successfully too, I might add. Why can't we make it work? And could you at least look at me?"

He finally turned to look at her, an expressionless wall hiding the unsettled, racing feeling in his chest.

Bracing her hands against the sides of her wheelchair, Samantha stood up and met him eye to eye, standing so close enough he could feel her breath against his face.

"Tell me now that I don't matter," she said in a soft voice. "Tell me that you can live without me."

"I didn't say that . . . Miss Weiss," he replied, his tone softer but still absent of inflection. "Any relationship I might desire would be a potential security risk to more than just myself."

"Then kiss me. Just one kiss to see if you really can walk away from what lies between us."

For a long, pregnant moment Agent Hessman said nothing and gazed into her loving, hopeful eyes. She made no move to physically urge or entice him. She simply stood there as if waiting for him to respond. When he drew in a long slow breath, Samantha's eyes brightened.

He gave her a curt nod and spoke in a level tone. "I fear I cannot afford the luxury. Good day, Miss Weiss."

Samantha stood with her hands braced against her wheelchair as a feeling of shock rolled through her. Tears welled.

Agent Hessman turned away and continued his walk down the hall.

CHAPTER EIGHTEEN
ASSEMBLING

AGENT HESSMAN, SUE HARRIS, DR. Sam Weiss, Ben, Claire, and Mr. Thomas assembled at the beginning of a new day in the middle of the control room. Notable for her absence was Samantha.

General Karlson stood at the central dais giving them and their supplies a final once-over. Sue wore a body suit with small pouches about her belt. Dr. Weiss carried his cane and a fanny pack for anything else he might need. Ben dressed in his usual baggy clothes, his deep pockets bulging with paraphernalia, and Agent Hessman wore a suit jacket designed to hide whatever he may be carrying. Mr. Thomas frowned like an accountant with a severe attitude.

Dressed in her usual flamboyant style, Claire stood out among them. General Karlson noted her white pants and blouse—totally inappropriate for any mission, but they made her long black hair stand out in contrast. She wore her trademark floppy white hat, and an oversized reporter's bag hung from one shoulder. Most of the team members seemed nervous or preoccupied, but Claire was nearly hopping with excitement.

"I get to interview an alien! This is the opportunity of a lifetime. Of several lifetimes. I spent all night just deciding what types of questions to ask."

"I have a few instruments with me," Dr. Weiss said, patting his fanny pack, "though I'm not sure how much good they'll do. We're more likely to encounter stuff beyond our capability to measure or even quantify."

"General," Agent Hessman said, "I'd like to take a better recording device along with me than just a cell phone, but I'm not sure how to sneak it past the aliens. Something to record audio, still pictures, film—the works—but I'm not sure how to hide it."

"Easy answer," Claire shrugged. "Don't." She reached into her bag and pulled out her reporter's badge, which she pinned to the front of her blouse. Then she removed a full-sized digital camera with a large and rather obvious lens attached. "I'm a reporter. Everyone knows it, so why hide it?"

"As usual," Ben said with a grin, "my wife has her own answer to the situation."

Claire hung the camera about her neck by its strap. She checked a readout at the back of her camera and pursed her lips with delight. "Can you believe it?" she said. "This thing can hold over a hundred pictures and record an hour or so of video. That's a far cry from what we had to work with a hundred years ago."

Her statement held a far more precise meaning for those who knew about her origins.

"Final check, everyone," the general announced. "The alien is due any moment. Make sure you are each prepared."

"What about you?" Dr. Weiss asked Sue. "You don't look like you're carrying much."

"I have what I need," Sue replied. "Expandable staff in my left-side belt pouch, various types of gas pellets in another pouch, a gun for their security to find hidden by my left hip, another small single-shot pistol by my right ankle, a pair of brass knuckles which they might think harmless, a small plastic tube in case I need to blow darts or a spit-wad or something at someone, and a couple of small trackers to stick on someone if required."

"You sound ready, as usual," Dr. Weiss smiled. "But what if they don't allow any of your weapons inside?"

Sue tilted her head slightly to one side. "I *am* a weapon," she replied in a tone that suggested what she said should have been obvious.

"And you?" Agent Hessman asked Mr. Thomas. "Do you have everything you'll need on you?"

"Classified," he replied.

General Karlson nodded.

Claire had just pointed her camera at the team for a few pictures when Sonsa Tabbak simply materialized in a brief flicker of light.

Several technicians, including Jason, jumped up from their seats. The general stepped back in surprise, wishing he could just appear like that at will. He noticed somewhat different reactions from his alien expedition team.

Dr. Weiss looked curious, as though he might be more interested in the manner of the alien's ability to materialize than in the alien itself. Sue cast a studied eye across the alien, as though she were searching for potential weak spots. Agent Hessman looked completely unperturbed, Mr. Thomas scowled, Ben watched on curiously, while Claire snapped a quick picture of the alien.

Jason sat down again and leaned toward his neighbor. "They act like they see aliens appearing out of thin air all the time," he whispered.

"They've met futuristic time travelers with personal cloaking devices and advanced tech," the other technician whispered back. "They probably do."

Claire snapped another picture of the alien, then let the camera drop around her neck as she took out a small palm-sized recording stick to hold up before him.

"Mr. Sonsa Tabbak—is that Mr. or Miss? Or do you have another pronoun I should be using?"

"There is no need for either since 'Sonsa' itself is a title that means 'Commander.'"

"Then I've actually been calling you Mr. Commander Tabbak," Claire said with a light giggle. "How silly of me, I'm sorry."

"The error is understandable, Miss Hill-Stein."

"Please, just Claire. Hill-Stein is my byline. Claire is my name among friends. We are friends, aren't we?"

"That," the alien said with a faint flicker of a smile, "is what this meeting will determine."

"And how often do you meet with worlds such as our own?" Claire asked, raising her microphone closer to the tall alien. "Is there a standard procedure you use for first-contact situations?"

"We have procedures," he stated. "Though yours is not a standard situation."

"Because of the time travel aspect," Claire replied. "I see. And how often does your own race travel through time? I'm guessing you're pretty good at it from the way you straightened out our mess. Or would that be a state secret?"

General Karlson was beginning to realize that Claire had the ability to dig out answers to many difficult questions.

"It would, Miss Hill-Stein," Sonsa Tabbak replied. "Now, if you are all ready—"

"A couple more questions, please. Will we be meeting other types of aliens or just your own species? You mentioned that 'Sonsa' is actually your rank. Does your clothing have any special designation? You're wearing a gold jumpsuit with a blue cape, for example. Is any of that some sort of rank insignia?"

"The color of my jumpsuit indicates what branch I work in, while the cape signifies my rank as a commander. Now if you are ready?"

To this rapid barrage of questions, Mr. Thomas leaned into Agent Hessman for a quick, quiet word. "I see why you bring her along on your missions. She's a combination diplomat and CIA interrogation team. I know of a secret agency or two that wouldn't mind signing her on."

"Sorry, but she's all ours," Agent Hessman replied.

"You will have plenty of opportunity to ask questions and take more pictures once we are on my vessel," Sonsa Tabbak stated to Claire.

"Oh, of course," Claire replied. She put the microphone back in her bag and then stood beside Ben. She flashed a grin at the alien.

The alien replied with a polite nod, then raised his right hand. A quick flicker of light expanded out from him to include the entire team. Only the briefest of moments, but once it was gone, so were the alien and Agent Hessman's team.

This time the general didn't jump. He simply looked at the empty space where they had been and said two words. "Good luck."

CHAPTER NINETEEN
TRIP TO AN ALIEN WORLD

THEY ARRIVED IN THE SAME room Agent Hessman had seen before, with the scanner tunnel before them. The room held the Americans, the Chinese delegation, the Russian delegation, Sonsa Tabbak and a couple more aliens. Five Chinese—one woman and four males, five Russians—all male, and their own six, made for a reasonably crowded room.

Claire immediately began working her camera, snapping pictures of everything and everyone, including the other two teams.

"The tunnel through that archway over there"—Agent Hessman pointed—"is basically like an airport scanner. It will scan us for weapons and pathogens."

"A sensible precaution," Dr. Weiss noted. "Well, who's first?"

"Me, of course," Sue said, stepping forward. "Sorry, Lou, but it's not my job to take anyone's word on this thing's safety."

"Understood," Agent Hessman replied. "Proceed."

As Sue walked towards the tunnel, one of the Russians stepped in front of her. "A good Russian does not permit a woman to step into danger before him," the man stated. "I will go first."

THE ALIENS STEP IN

"You know, I can drop you in at least three different ways," she said with a glare.

"Ah ha!" He laughed, loud and bold. "A *real* woman. If you are not Russian, you should be! Andros Kortnev, at your service. And you?"

"Your better," she said, stepping past him.

The remark got another grin from the Russian.

Sue proceeded through the scanner. When the first chute opened, she dropped a pistol inside. Midway through, when the force field stopped her and another chute popped up, she unstrapped the other pistol from her ankle with a sigh, and she dropped it into the chute, followed by her expandable staff and gas pellets. Only then did the force field drop and let her continue.

Next the Russian, Andros Kortnev, stepped up. He barely got one step through when a light shone on his right pants pocket and a force field stopped him. With a grin, he took out a small bottle filled with a clear liquid.

"What is that?" Sonsa Tabbak asked.

"This is vodka," the Russian replied. "I was going to give it to your leader, maybe toast our friendship."

"A kind offer," the alien replied, "but we will have to determine if it is poisonous to our kind first."

"It is poisonous to *our* kind," Andros laughed, "but that doesn't stop us from drinking it."

Sonsa Tabbak stepped back to confer briefly with another alien before giving a nod to the Russian. The force field disappeared, and Andros was able to continue with his walk.

It went on like that, each of the humans in turn stepping through the scanner, some more cautiously than others.

All the while, Agent Hessman kept a careful eye on everyone—Russians, Chinese, and aliens alike. He was suspicious of all of them, but as the process continued, he took particular note of Sonsa Tabbak. For it seemed that while the alien was keeping just as cautious an eye on all three groups of humans, he was keeping particular watch on the Chinese delegation—a fact that had Agent Hessman paying greater attention to the Chinese as well.

The Chinese woman in particular seemed a bit twitchy. Agent Hessman suspected her nervousness might be due to something more than just the presence of aliens in an alien environment. When it came time for the woman to take the walk through the scanner, Agent Hessman saw one of her hands shaking.

Immediately, the scanner flashed once. A transparent force field snapped into place before the Chinese woman, and a light shone onto one of her coat pockets.

Agent Hessman watched intently and wondered what Sonsa Tabbak would be thinking. He did not have to wait long.

"You have something there," Sonsa Tabbak flatly stated to the woman. "We must see it."

"N-nothing dangerous, really," she replied in heavily accented English.

To the alien's leveling look, she reached into her pocket and pulled out a syringe.

"Insulin," she told them. "For my diabetes. Really, I'm just a researcher. Dr. Cissy Wang. I have diabetes and—"

A light shone on the injector momentarily, and the force field flicked off.

"The presence of insulin is confirmed," Sonsa Tabbak stated. "You may proceed."

Agent Hessman seemed satisfied when she was allowed to proceed.

With a nervous hand, Dr. Wang put the syringe away and continued her walk through the scanner. Once she was through, she let out a sigh of relief and joined the other members of her team.

Agent Hessman narrowed his gaze in her direction for a moment but said nothing.

Next came Claire. She snapped a picture of the scanner tunnel before stepping in, then took a couple more of the interior on her way through.

THE ALIENS STEP IN

Ben was next, more to stay close to his wife than anything else.

Agent Hessman took one last look around the room. When he was sure he was the last human in the room and only Sonsa Tabbak remained, he walked through the scanner with a focused gaze on those ahead of him.

Sonsa Tabbak followed. Once again, they were all gathered in the anteroom that gave admittance into the rest of the vessel.

"We will be taking a smaller craft to my home world while the main vessel stays in orbit about your world. What you would call the 'shuttle bay' is nearly two miles from here, but we have conveyances to take us there quicker," Sonsa Tabbak said.

"We aren't going to walk?" Andros asked, sounding nearly disappointed. "Two miles is small hike. You should try five miles through Russian winter."

"Sorry, my friend," Agent Hessman quipped. "Not everything can be as difficult as your countrymen seem to prefer it."

"You've been to Russia then?" Andros asked.

"I have some Russian colleagues who are very much at odds with their own opinions. They brag about Russian winters while hating it and love their vodka even as they complain about the taste."

"*Da*," the other man chuckled. "That is Russia. We are people of paradox."

"If you are all ready," Sonsa Tabbak announced, "please stay close and do not touch anything."

The panel slid open behind them, admitting them into a world that only Agent Hessman and Mr. Thomas had seen before.

Agent Hessman followed the others onto the familiar landing. However, this time the alien led them down the rightmost hall. Several of Sonsa Tabbak's kind wandered the pale blue hallway, each dressed in one of several colors of jumpsuits. Only Sonsa Tabbak wore a cape. The hallway appeared to continue for a long way with no exits in sight.

Claire began snapping pictures and pulled out her microphone. She popped a question to an alien dressed in a blue jumpsuit. "Excuse me, but

#9 – GALNARAN SHUTTLE CRAFT

I've recently learned that the color of your jumpsuit has some meaning. Could you tell me what field your color indicates?"

The alien glanced at her and continued on his way past the group.

"How long have you served on this ship?" Claire asked of another. "And what would a typical term of service be?"

"Fifty-four years so far," the alien answered on its way past.

"That's quite a long time," Claire remarked. She turned to Sonsa Tabbak. "How long *does* your species live?"

"I am six hundred of your years old, if you deem that answer enough," the alien replied.

"Six hundred. Wow!"

Their guide stopped suddenly before what appeared to be a blank wall. He laid a hand on it, and a hidden panel slid aside to reveal a room with a transparent far wall, although at present, it afforded them no more than a view of another wall. The room appeared to be just big enough to hold the delegation.

"Please enter," Sonsa motioned. "This conveyance will take us to where we need to go."

"It's an elevator," Ben realized. "A large elevator."

"Of a sort," the alien replied as the others followed Ben inside. "This moves horizontally as well as vertically. You may sit or stand as you desire."

The walls to either side, Agent Hessman now noticed, had benches built in. Like the room walls, the benches were of the same shade of bluish-white as the hallway.

Once they had all entered, the door slid closed behind them, and the view through the transparent wall started to move. They were moving—not that Agent Hessman could feel the motion.

"We will move through some of the engineering sections," Sonsa Tabbak explained. "You can see it through the transparency."

In a moment, the view changed from the inside of a tunnel to a view overlooking a deep valley of mechanization, much like what Agent Hessman had seen earlier. This time, however, he saw a lot more of it mixed with what looked like control stations. Floating sections of floor hovered before brightly glowing panels embedded in the side of multi-story equipment. Aliens stood on some of the floating floors and worked controls on those panels.

High above, Agent Hessman saw a bright green light reflecting down from some other unseen contraption of mammoth proportions. At the far end of the chamber, a craft about the size of a semi-truck was currently disemboweled. A multi-limbed, floating industrial robot worked over it. What looked like large capsules shot through the air at a safe range above the bulk of the taller structures.

Claire switched her camera from snapshot to film mode. Dr. Weiss found himself entranced with the complexity before him, as indeed were the Russian and Chinese teams. Agent Hessman was paying more attention to their reactions to the sights than he was to the alien technology itself.

"So many questions," Dr. Weiss remarked.

"So many security risks," Sue stated.

Indeed, Agent Hessman thought.

"Claire," Dr. Weiss asked, his eyes still fixed on the transparent wall, "I hope you'll do me the favor of granting me a copy of the video once we're back home."

"Of course," Claire replied.

"Such a woman," Andros remarked. "The rest of us like cavemen viewing automobile, while she still with mind on business. How can you stay so calm at such sights?"

"Simple," Claire said as she slowly panned her camera across the view. "I technically died a hundred years ago, so *everything* I've been seeing since I came to your modern times is to me what you're seeing out there."

The Russian looked puzzled for only a moment before he burst out in a chuckle.

Agent Hessman almost laughed.

They were nearly across the indoor expanse when the room angled downward, swooping smoothly a hundred feet lower before leveling out

THE ALIENS STEP IN

again. Agent Hessman swayed to keep his balance, as did everyone else on board. After that, they once again entered a tunnel, the transparent wall showing nothing but its inner wall.

"To see such things are possible," one of the Chinese contingent whispered to another. "Dr. Wang, what do you make of all this?"

Dr. Wang shook her head and remained silent. That the Chinese delegation had specifically singled her out for an expert opinion was reason enough for Agent Hessman to pay closer to her. The fact that Sonsa Tabbak's telepathic field was present and still acting as translator—just like it had on his previous visit—was not one that he currently cared to remind the Chinese delegation about.

When the room came to a full stop, the door panel once again slid silently aside behind Sonsa Tabbak as he motioned them out. "This is our shuttle launch bay. You will follow."

Claire was the first one out, still filming.

Agent Hessman waited until the others exited. Then he followed them onto the floor of what indeed looked to be some sort of launch bay, but of far larger proportions than any human had seen. The ceiling rose at least three stories, and the room stretched a thousand feet wide and twice that long. Several objects that looked like fifty-foot-long, silvery cigars hovered a foot above the deck, some tended by those multi-limbed industrial robots. More aliens walked the floor undertaking various duties.

"Mr. Tabbak, do we have enough time for me to interview a few of your friends around here?" Claire asked.

Ben put his finger to her chin and gently turned her head towards where the rest of the delegation was currently looking.

The far-right wall of the bay was completely absent, replaced by a faintly glimmering wall of nearly transparent silvery light. It was not the force field itself that had the group's collective attention, Agent Hessman thought, but what lay beyond it: space. Nothing but empty black void punctuated by the speckling of stars untainted by atmospheric attenuation or the curvature of a camera lens. Stars, space, and in the field of view below, the earth. Its western hemisphere was just turning into the light of the sun.

"By jeepers," Claire gasped.

"Jeepers?" Ben asked.

"I'm trying to catch up on my slang," she replied. "I'm only up to about the late forties right now."

"Then 'by jeepers' it is," Ben quietly agreed.

"This way, everyone," Sonsa Tabbak instructed.

Again, Hessman let the others go first. They followed Sonsa Tabbak in a silence punctuated only by the sound of footsteps and the soft click of Claire's camera.

As they approached one of the silvery cigars, a hatch started opening.

"The trip will not take long," the alien told them. "Only moments, in fact."

"Moments to cross the stars?" Dr. Weiss marveled. "And in such a small craft? How is such a thing possible?"

Agent Hessman hoped it would be as smooth a ride as their last transport.

"We will use a wormhole," Sonsa Tabbak answered. "The mothership has a wormhole generator."

"So, it opens up the wormhole, and this little craft simply rides it through," Dr. Weiss summarized.

"Correct," the alien replied. "That is why the shuttle can be so small. It has no main drive of its own, only a local drive good for no more than fifteen percent the speed of light."

"*Only* about fifteen percent light-speed?" Dr. Weiss marveled. He turned to Ben. "He said that with such a straight face."

The interior of the craft was little more than a nearly empty oval chamber paneled floor to ceiling in what looked like a mirror—except it cast nothing of their reflections. Empty, but for a panel at one end. Once everyone was inside, the alien placed a hand to the panel's surface. Although the panel had no controls Agent Hessman could see, with the alien's action, the door sealed shut. It became one with the rest of the wall. Then Agent

Hessman felt a slight sense of motion.

The alien glanced back at his charges. "If you will permit me a small pleasure, this is my favorite part of first contact encounters."

"What do you mean?" Mr. Thomas asked suspiciously.

"I mean, welcome to space." Sonsa Tabbak swept his six-fingered hand about the room.

In that moment, the silvery interior flickered away, enveloping the passengers in a full all-around view of what lay outside. Distantly below one side of the massive alien vessel, Agent Hessman saw the large blue sphere of Earth. An infinity of space and stars spanned every direction, with Agent Hessman and his fellow passengers afloat in its midst.

Even Andros the Russian was struck silent.

"Note to self," Claire voiced into her microphone. "Wow."

A glimmer of a smile crossed the alien's face before he got back to business. "Our next stop will be Galnar," he announced.

Agent Hessman snapped out of his astonished trance. He noted the fact that their new surroundings included two massive parallel bars, each a thousand feet long and a dozen feet thick, spaced just far enough apart for their shuttle to hover between them. The presence of those bars became even more pronounced when they began to glow brighter with every passing second.

"Quantum transporters," Sonsa Tabbak stated. "Now, observe. This is what the inside of a wormhole looks like."

As the two quantum transporters charged up, their dim glow expanded into a brightness rivaling that of the sun. A rainbow of colors spanned the distance between them, weaving bands of color around their shuttle, holding it tight. Infinity rushed to meet them, colliding with the ends of the quantum transporters until all the light in the Universe seemed collected there. Hessman felt no sense of movement at all. As that wall of light raced down the length of the twin quantum transporters directly toward them, the massive alien ship behind the shuttle dissolved into a distant point.

One of the Chinese contingent screamed. Andros and two of his

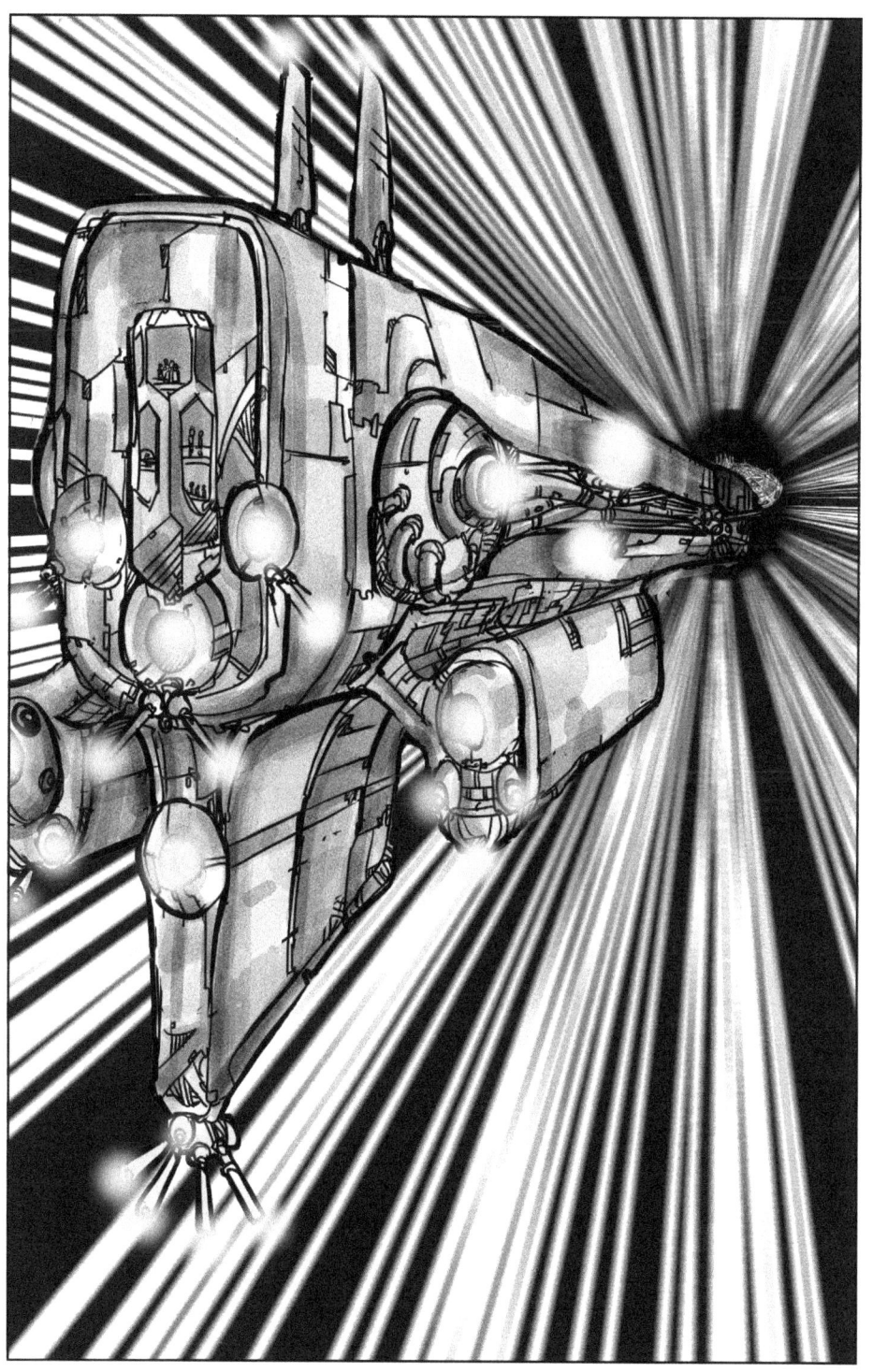

companions shouted Russian expletives. Agent Hessman quickly checked on his team. Sue held ready for anything, and Claire held a hand tight to Ben with her ever-ready-camera raised and filming. Mr. Thomas was intently observing the Chinese. Dr. Weiss was mesmerized by all of the new technology around him.

Down the space spanned by the quantum transporters the wall of light shot, until it passed right through the small vessel and the vessel through it. Within a flash of light, it was done.

Agent Hessman gasped. They were no longer above Earth.

And Claire's camera had recorded every instant of the event.

CHAPTER TWENTY

ARRIVAL

"WELCOME TO GALNAR," SONSA TABBAK announced. Agent Hessman glanced around him. Before them floated a planetary orb. While not quite as large as Earth, it was definitely alien in its completely foreign display of continents, oceans, and cloud patterns. Galnar had two suns, just as the alien had told them.

"It . . . it's blue," one of the Chinese contingent exclaimed. "Like Earth."

"You expected your world to be the only one with oceans and water?" Sonsa Tabbak remarked. "Our gravity is lower, and we have no night, but other than that, you might find some similarities. Now, enjoy the view while I fly us over to the Hall of Governance."

Down through the cloud cover they flew. Agent Hessman kept his eyes pinned to the transparent walls in an attempt to get the first glimpse of what sights the alien world might hold. Swiftly, they descended through one layer of clouds after another until the last cloud cleared away, giving the shuttle's passengers their first view of Galnar's surface.

The ocean shimmered greenish blue along one edge of a mountainous land sparkling with bluish snow. Stretching across the valley below, however,

#11 – Galnar from Space

were cities that defined Galnar as an alien land. As they fell through the sky, Agent Hessman marveled at needle-like structures towering half a mile high, built from a shiny blue and white material that glistened like ceramic. Other squatter structures rolled for miles across the landscape. They looked like artificial snow-capped hills with the same blue and white sheen. As the craft drew closer, Agent Hessman saw other silvery craft like their own flitting through the sky. He looked down. There were no roads as none were needed. Instead, there was just a loose tangle of walkways for those afoot.

Building tops glittered in the twin sunlight, some sparking with energy that ran down the length of the given tower and then grounded into the soil. In all, they were a glittering tribute to the alien hands that had designed them.

One building in particular caught Agent Hessman's attention. It was one of the squatter ones but of an exceptionally large size. With mile-high spires at each of its apexes, its outer perimeter resembled a twelve-point star.

"That building looks to be at *least* three miles across," Dr. Weiss gasped, pointing. "And those spires!"

Andros exclaimed something in Russian that the alien's telepathic field did not translate. Then he turned to the Americans. "Oh, please excuse. How would you say it in English?"

"I'm stuck with 'wow' myself," Claire shrugged.

"Too weak a word," Andros replied.

"By the gods," one of the Chinese contingent exclaimed at the sight.

"Getting closer," Andros said.

"What are we looking at?" Agent Hessman asked.

"The city below is Setra, our capital," Sonsa Tabbak explained. "The large structure that has you all so enthralled is the Hall of Governance, which is where we will be meeting with our supreme leader, Qual Ahk-Sonsa Kadahth. That translates roughly to—"

"Supreme Leader Kadahth?" Claire suggested.

"Exactly so," the alien replied. "A very good guess, Miss Hill-Stein."

"I catch on quickly," she replied. "Good survival trait for any reporter

and time traveler."

"Kadahth is the Supreme Leader of the Interstellar Union based in

Setra, here on our world of Galnar," Sonsa Tabbak explained. "We must go directly to the Hall of Governance for a very important meeting with him, but I am slowing the craft to give you time to acclimate to the sights."

"And ask questions," Claire said, immediately skipping over to the alien's side. "For instance, that wormhole thing you used to zap us across half the galaxy—"

"We are in what you call Orion's Belt."

"Yeah, well, how often do you use those wormholes to get around? Was this just a special emergency, or do you use them the way we use cars and such?" Claire pressed.

"Fascinating," Dr. Weiss stated.

"What about environmental effects?" Dr. Weiss added.

Agent Hessman held his tongue. The others were doing a good job o raising the questions on his mind.

"I would be interested in how you generate such things," Dr. Cissy Wang asked. "And what is the weapon potential for these wormholes?"

The walls remained transparent as their descent slowed above the city. The whole of their view was reminiscent of a jewel carved from ice.

Shadows cast from the twin suns were displayed as overlapping rainbows that twisted about one another.

"I will say, Mrs. Hill-Stein, that we are able to generate wormholes as needed, and we do use them often to travel long-distances." Sonsa Tabbak turned to Dr. Weiss. "As far as environmental effects are concerned, that is a very good question, Dr. Weiss, but in the end, not a consideration. Wormholes are erected in a collimated form from one point to another, and only for very brief times, which completely eliminates any residual effects. Of course, we only use them when outside the range of a planet's atmosphere."

"Does that mean using a wormhole within an atmosphere could constitute a weapon?" Dr. Wang asked.

#13 – City of Setra

Agent Hessman suspiciously narrowed his gaze at Dr. Wang. He noticed that Sonsa Tabbak did the same. The alien was certainly astute.

"I understand Dr. Wang's question after seeing that ghost town you incinerated," Dr. Weiss interjected between jaw-dropping views of the alien city. "We've been trying to figure out how you did it."

"We have the ability to dissociate matter into its base components," Sonsa Tabbak replied with a shrug. "But we can also reverse that process, creating any desired material in any desired form from base components."

"Any type of matter?" Dr. Wang persisted.

The alien again fixed the woman with a brief look before replying.

"There are some limits," the alien admitted. "For instance, we cannot create life this way. The structure of DNA and other biological components is simply too complex for that process."

"Ah," Dr. Wang again interjected. "Then there *are* limits to your technology. Ways in which one may defend against it."

Sonsa Tabbak gave the woman a long last look before turning his eye back to Claire. "I like your questions better. Ask what you wish."

"Great," the reporter beamed. "Let's start with the basics. Sex. Do your people have male and female sexes, or do you have something else going on?"

Agent Hessman gasped, along with several others in the room.

"Claire!" exclaimed a shocked Ben.

"What? If he's all that advanced, why would he care about answering? And here I thought that *I* was the one from the prudish early twentieth century. Well, Mr. Tabbak?"

Agent Hessman was concerned about the reaction to Claire's questions. He knew from prior experience that Claire was her own person and would ask almost anything.

"I do not mind answering," the alien replied before anyone else could object. "We have long since abandoned the pursuit of any physical pleasures, such as sex, eating for enjoyment, and so on. Sex is for procreating and nothing more."

"Then where *do* you get your pleasure from?" Claire continued. "For if you don't get pleasure from something, then why live at all?"

"A very astute deduction, Miss Hill-Stein. We focus ourselves on the pleasure gained from discovery and intellectual pursuits.

"In our most recent endeavor, we made contact with intelligent life in other dimensions," Sonsa Tabbak continued. "We look forward to developing the ability to move freely between our dimension and countless others. Exploring other dimensions to expand our knowledge is of significant interest to us. We also derive a great deal of pleasure from art and music."

"Art! That's the angle," Claire decided.

"Can we see any examples of your alien art?" Claire asked.

"We're passing over one work of art right now." He pointed through the clear floor to something in an open square that looked like a public fountain. No water flowed from it, but rather, standing designs carved in light. "That is a light sculpture."

"Like a hologram?" Ben asked.

"Only in the most general sense, Professor Stein. We also have concerts."

"Alien singing?" Claire nearly bounced on her feet. "Can we hear a sample of some of your singing? Please?"

"It may lose a little something to your ears, but I can call up a recording of a recent operatic piece." One webbed hand passed over a small section of the control panel, and then, alien singing arose all around. It was a discordant assembly of notes with random chord progressions, uneven pauses, and generally disagreeable vocalizations. After a few moments, with elements of all three delegations making faces, Sonsa Tabbak shut the music off with another sweep of his webbed hand.

"Not wanting to be rude," one of the Russians stated, "but that sounded awful."

"I said it would lose something to your ears," Sonsa Tabbak reminded them. "Your ears cannot hear the ultrasonic notes that my species is capable of singing."

"So, this is more in the range of what a dog might listen to," Sue ventured.

"Music fit for a dog," Andros chuckled. "Not meaning to offend, but it *is* funny."

The alien paused for a brief moment to consider, then nodded. "Agreed. Now, if you will all prepare yourselves, we have arrived at the Hall of Governance."

The view through the walls showed them drifting down to a smooth landing atop the roof of the largest squat building, the one encircled with spires. As the shuttle touched down, its walls became solid once again. In another moment, with an accompanying sense of change of motion, a wave of Sonsa Tabbak's hand over the control panel caused the door to slide open once again.

"Please be careful stepping out," Sonsa Tabbak advised. "I would not want your first steps on our world to be tragic ones."

Claire nearly skipped out through the opening, while Agent Hessman held a more cautious eye over disembarking passengers.

CHAPTER TWENTY-ONE
INTERROGATION

AGENT HESSMAN ALLOWED THE OTHERS to the exit before stepping out onto a surface like textured glass, where hot winds whipped playfully about his face. The craft had landed in the middle of the roof, an area festooned with tubes and robotic limbs that were already connecting into the craft for whatever maintenance it was their job to perform.

Another alien awaited them. This one was dressed in a greenish jumpsuit and no cape. Other craft were about, some landing, others lifting off, each tended to by other devices and other Galnarans. Each landed craft, including their own, was tethered next to an eight-foot needle that sparked with energy.

"I am named Tahsa Ray'ahl," said the Galnarian in the capeless green jumpsuit. "I am to escort you to the waiting room until Supreme Leader Kadahth is ready to meet with you."

"Then we aren't going directly to him?" Dr. Wang asked.

"He is very busy," Tahsa Ray'ahl answered. "This is standard procedure. Now, if you will follow me."

As Tahsa Ray'ahl began to lead the way across the landing-pad roof, Sonsa Tabbak quickly approached him. They shared a few words in their

tongue—words which no one else could understand.

Agent Hessman glanced at Claire, who responded with a slight nod, confirming that they were being recorded for later examination.

As the two aliens spoke, Sonsa Tabbak brought out the Chinese temporal radiation detector and showed it to Tahsa Ray'ahl.

Agent Hessman eyed the Chinese to observe their reactions. They simply acted as if the alien exchange held no real importance—as if the device were just another piece of equipment like Agent Hessman's cell phone. He narrowed his eyes, believing the truth about the Chinese device was far more important than they let on. He had been suspicious of them from the beginning. They were much more devious than the Russians.

Tahsa Ray'ahl finally brought the group to a halt in the middle of the tarmac with no portal in sight—at least until the ground gently shook beneath their feet. Agent Hessman realized they were slowly moving downward.

Turning to the Chinese, Tahsa Ray'ahl held up the temporal radiation detector that Sonsa Tabbak had shown him. He asked the obvious question: "Where did you get this device?"

Agent Hessman leaned toward the Chinese, eager to hear their response. But they exchanged looks and said nothing. He looked up. They had now descended thirty feet beneath the roof, and the tarmac was sliding closed overhead. The only available light came softly from the walls around them.

"I will ask again," Tahsa Ray'ahl said to the Chinese delegation. "Where did you obtain this device?"

Again, no answer.

The floor suddenly stopped, but no door opened in response.

"Our kind can go seven days without food and water," Sonsa Tabbak said. "And we are very patient. This room will remain here, closed, until we have answers. Now, where did you get it from?"

"Starving us out until we talk," Mr. Thomas muttered. "Nice interrogation method."

Agent Hessman glared at him.

The Chinese exchanged silent looks. Then Dr. Wang stepped forward. "I designed it."

"Impossible," Tahsa Ray'ahl replied. "Where did you get it? Keep in mind that we have activated technology that will monitor your surface thoughts to determine if you lie or not. Answer."

"I designed it myself," Dr. Cissy Wang insisted. "I am . . . brilliant."

Agent Hessman raised an eyebrow.

The two aliens exchanged looks then seemed to come to some hesitant agreement.

"You speak true," Tahsa Ray'ahl decided. "Though it makes no sense." He turned to the Russian contingent. "You. What do you know of this device made by your cousins?"

"The Chinese are no cousins of ours," Andros replied. "And if we knew how, do you not think that we'd be making our own?"

Tahsa Ray'ahl paused for a moment, as if listening to something. "Again, the truth."

"As far as he is saying," Sonsa Tabbak added. "Some of these Earthers appear quite skilled in saying nothing while speaking much."

Andros grinned.

Dr. Wang lifted up her chin with a measure of pride.

Then the aliens turned to Agent Hessman.

"What do you know of the history of this device?" Tahsa Ray'ahl asked.

"We found it on a Chinese agent on a recent trip to the past," Agent Hessman replied. "We were hoping that you could tell us a little more. How did the Chinese make it? I have a greater interest in that answer than you do. The way you so easily recognize the technology, I'm thinking that perhaps you're the ones holding back information—information more directly vital to our survival than yours."

The aliens did not respond.

"Well?" Agent Hessman met the alien's gaze for a long moment before Tahsa Ray'ahl turned to Sonsa Tabbak with a query on his own face. Apparently, it was more of their nonverbal communication.

Sonsa Tabbak shrugged.

"Perhaps we shall ask another delegate," Tahsa Ray'ahl said, looking at Sue. "Agent Sue Harris, what do you know about the Chinese efforts into time travel? How extensive are your own?"

"Surface thoughts, right?" she said. "And you can only tell if what we say is true or not?"

Tahsa Ray'ahl nodded.

"Okay then," Sue continued. "Lou is our team leader and speaks for all of us. If we had one of those gizmos, we wouldn't have been trying to get it from the Chinese. And my favorite color is red."

Tahsa Ray'ahl studied her for a moment and grinned. "I can sense your lie," he said.

"You're right," Sue replied blandly. "My favorite color is blue. Sometimes green."

The alien's grin turned into a frown. Sue responded with a sly smile of her own.

Before the aliens could confer once again, however, Claire spoke up. "Look, we're getting off on the wrong foot. What we need is an icebreaker, a little give and take."

"What would you suggest?" Tahsa Ray'ahl asked.

"Something to build trust and make everyone feel more at ease. For instance, tell us a little bit about yourselves, your people. How long have you been traveling in space? You've obviously been watching us, but for how long? Have you ever really been to Earth before?"

Inwardly, Agent Hessman smiled. The reporter was, once again, asking questions that he would like to know the answers to.

Claire held out her microphone with a hopeful expression. The two aliens exchanged looks and shrugged.

Then Tahsa Ray'ahl spoke. "Our history of space travel goes back tens of thousands of years. It has become as standard to us as driving a car is to you."

"Oh, come on," Claire responded. "How can space travel ever be considered that bland with all that must be out there? You must still come across something new every day."

"That is true," Sonsa Tabbak calmly replied. "It is one of the things that spurs our delight in life."

"I can just imagine," Claire sighed. "To be able to roam the stars... you must love it."

"We do," Tahsa Ray'ahl said. "And we have been to your world before. About four thousand years ago."

Agent Hessman frowned. He realized the aliens knew a lot about Earthers. That realization disturbed him.

"You have?" Ben perked up. "Exactly when? Oh! Sorry to cut in, but history is my field. It's what got me interested in time travel, to see the past firsthand."

"That is what we use it for as well," Tahsa Ray'ahl admitted. "As any species, we have many questions about our own distant past, as well as the past of others. It helps us to understand other concerns, such as human behavior, even more."

As the conversation continued, Andros approached Agent Hessman.

"The woman has advance degree in psychology, yes?" Andros asked.

"Not that I'm aware of," Agent Hessman replied quietly. "Although I can see how you might make that assumption."

"That brings up a pertinent question," Tahsa Ray'ahl asked, turning to the Russians. "Your American companion has said that he became interested in time travel out of intellectual curiosity, but what about the rest of you? Why do you risk the dangers of time travel?"

"If they do it, then we have to as well," Andros shrugged. "It keeps balance."

"Don't look at me," Sue said as the alien gaze panned round the group, "I'm just the muscle. And please don't ask Dr. Weiss. He'll go on for hours on the details of his intellectual curiosity, and by then, I'm sure your supreme leader will have gone to bed."

"And what of you," Tahsa Ray'ahl turned now to the Chinese contingent. "Dr. Wang, what of time travel interests you?"

"As the American said," she replied evenly, "I am interested in history as well."

Once again, the aliens exchanged quizzical looks. Then Tahsa Ray'ahl handed the Chinese temporal radiation detector back to Sonsa Tabbak. "She speaks her truth," Tahsa Ray'ahl announced. "The telepathic monitor confirms she does not lie."

With that announcement, the room gave the slightest lurch and started its downward movement once more. As satisfied as the aliens looked to be, however, Agent Hessman was doubtful. It must have shown on his face; Mr. Thomas motioned him off to one side.

"Assessment?" Mr. Thomas asked.

Agent Hessman glanced at Dr. Wang before whispering his reply. "I can think of several ways her statement could hide the truth and not register as a lie. I don't care how advanced these aliens may be, I still trust my gut more than their psychic monitors."

"Agreed," Mr. Thomas replied.

The room stopped and one wall slid aside.

"The waiting room." Tahsa Ray'ahl said. He stepped into another room with blue and white tinged walls, and he motioned the rest to follow. "Qual Ahk-Sonsa Kadahth will see you when he is ready."

They entered a brightly lit chamber that held little save a large set of double doors that were currently closed and guarded by a pair of brown robed Galnarans.

"Be warned," Sonsa Tabbak stated, gesturing to the double-doors. "Those doors will not open until it is time for your audience. Please be patient."

After the new arrivals entered the waiting room and separated into their respective delegations, Tahsa Ray'ahl and Sonsa Tabbak left through the set of double doors to confer with their intended audience, leaving the three groups of humans to themselves.

Agent Hessman kept an eye on everyone, with particular attention to Dr. Wang.

CHAPTER TWENTY-TWO
WAITING ROOM

"APPARENTLY THESE ALIENS HAVE NO respect for a man with a cane," Dr. Weiss remarked as they waited.

"You'd think there would be at least one chair, a bench, or something to sit on," Agent Hessman agreed.

Indeed, the room was unfurnished and unadorned, leaving everyone to stand and wait under the watchful eye of the Galnaran guards. The room was circular, so with no corners to huddle against, the Chinese delegates picked one section away from the others, while the Russian delegates and Agent Hessman's team each found their own spots.

"Sam," Ben said, "you know you don't need that cane anymore than I do. You said it yourself, it's just for appearances now."

"And that look would include being offered a seat in a nice plush chair," Dr. Weiss stated. "Maybe a smoking jacket and a wide snifter of brandy."

"Alien planet, remember," Ben told him.

"Well, there is that" Sam admitted. "They may have by far the greater technology, but we may have to educate them on social graces."

"As advanced as these aliens obviously are," Ben said, "I don't think we have a thing to teach them."

"Don't we?" Sam replied with a slight grin. "No matter how advanced a given society is, they always lack something that they can learn from so-called more primitive societies. As evidence, I present your own wife. From a hundred years back, and yet we are constantly learning things from her."

Ben looked about to say something, eyed Claire, and stopped to think it over.

"Go ahead," Claire said, "say anything."

Ben shrugged, gave his wife a peck on the cheek. "I admit to being verbally outmaneuvered and concede the point."

As those three carried on their conversation, Sue stood by Agent Hessman's side, keeping a wary eye on the other groups of humans. Mr. Thomas kept an eye on both Agent Hessman and the aliens.

"Assessment," Agent Hessman whispered to Sue. "Aliens first."

"I could probably take one of them in a strictly physical fight," she answered. "But with their technology they'd have me on the floor before I could reach them. At least two of the Chinese are trained bodyguards—their version of me. As for the Russians, as long as one of them is not a *Spetsnoz,* I'm good."

"I'm more worried about motives," Agent Hessman replied. "Mr. Thomas here simply makes the broad assumption of not trusting anyone, but I need something more concrete."

"The aliens don't need any subterfuge," Sue shrugged. "They have us vastly overpowered and at their mercy. The Chinese I would never trust simply on general principles. As for the Russians, well, one of them is coming over here now, so I guess you could ask him yourself."

Indeed, Andros Kortnev approached with a big smile and an arm poised to either slap someone on the back or connect with a forearm greeting.

"My friends!" He grinned broadly. "And for once, we surely must be friends, for we are all on the same side, no?" He looked as though he were about to slap his hand to Sue's back, caught the glare in her eyes, and stopped the motion midway through. Instead, he elected to offer his hand.

Agent Hessman stepped forward to shake it. "I'm Special Agent Lou Hessman."

Still clutching Agent Hessman's hand, the Russian drew him a bit closer. "Ah, you sound like my counterpart then. I guessed correct. And the young woman here?"

"Sharp blow to your third vertebrae," Sue blandly responded. "Double kidney punch from the back, groin shot with my knee—always a favorite—and a haymaker coming up from beneath the chin."

"Excuse me?" the Russian asked.

"Some of the ways I can incapacitate you in a single shot. I'm Agent Sue Harris."

"Russian foreplay." Andros grinned and turned to Mr. Thomas. "And what about you? Permit me for saying so, but you don't look like much."

"I'm the man whom no one wants to mess with," Mr. Thomas snapped back. "I take it this is more than a social visit?"

"Yes, I see, well..." Andros lowered his voice, stepping closer to Agent Hessman. While still wearing a smile, his voice grew far more serious. He glanced once over his shoulder in the direction of the Chinese before continuing. "Mr. Hessman, I notice that you do not seem to trust the Chinese anymore than I do. And yet the alien technology says they told the truth."

"I know a handful of ways in which any lie detector can be fooled, even alien ones," Agent Hessman replied. "Their technology, as advanced as it is, is still no better than the ones using it."

"Your gut says they lie, as does mine," Andros stated. "I think the aliens suspect it too, but do not know how to prove it."

"On that we agree," Agent Hessman replied. "If I had access to the alien equipment, I would probe deeper into some of their thoughts. Particularly that Dr. Cissy Wang. Unfortunately, I am not able to use any of my regular interrogation methods."

"Lou, I know some of those methods, and they leave a little to be desired."

Agent Hessman turned at the sound of Claire's voice. She, Ben, and Dr.

Weiss had joined them.

"You have another method, Miss Hill-Stein?" Agent Hessman asked. "Perhaps something more subtle?"

"What's subtle? I'm a reporter." She straightened her press badge, reached into her reporter's bag, pulled out her digital camera, and headed for the Chinese delegation with a broad smile on her face.

The fake smile fell from Andros's face as he faced Agent Hessman with a concerned question.

"The woman is naïve, yes? Is not so simple."

"I have learned never to underestimate her," Agent Hessman replied.

"My wife will probably come back with complete dossiers on every member of that group before Sonsa Tabbak returns." Ben grinned. "And she'll make friends with at least one of them."

The Russian looked doubtfully at Claire's retreat as she walked up to the nearest member of the Chinese group and stuffed her mic into his face.

"Excuse me, but my name is Claire Hill-Stein, and I was wondering if you would answer a few questions for the record."

"Claire Hill?" The man's expression immediately jumped from one of suspicion to that of a kid meeting Santa Claus. "The same one from a hundred years ago?"

"The very same," she smiled. "But how could you know about me?"

"I've read all your articles," the man replied.

"Me too," another Chinese delegate said. "I love the way you get around some of those situations."

"Why, thank you!" Claire smiled, performing a quick curtsey. "But those articles are all classified."

Good, Agent Hessman thought. *She's digging.*

The man Claire was speaking to lowered his eyes with a guilty look. "I may have peeked into a couple of the papers circulating out from the foreign intelligence ministry."

"Everyone has seen them," the second man added. "They are favorite things to read. Very exciting."

"How do you like that?" Claire remarked. "I'm a world-famous reporter amongst all the better spy agencies. So, what do you think of the aliens' offer? Do you think they have any ulterior motives?"

"Everyone has ulterior motives," the first man said with a shrug. "They mention 'gift,' but I think it is more to lure us to give up our time-technology program."

"And you think that would not be a fair exchange?" Claire pressed. "After all, I can say from personal experience how dangerous time technology can be."

"Our time technology is vastly superior to American or Russian efforts," a third Chinese delegate said. "Would not be fair trade."

"Superior, you say," Claire said, moving her mic over to the third man.

Agent Hessman strained his eyes to listen. Report? Agent? Claire certainly had a gift for grilling interview subjects.

"Yet my sources say that you merely stole your technology from the American project. How do you respond to that?" Claire continued.

"It was that way at first," the man shrugged. "Oh, my name is Li Wei. You spell that *l-i, w-e-i*. Are you going to take pictures? Will my picture be in your article?"

"I'll take a group shot when I'm finished," Claire told him. "But you said, 'at first.'"

"Oh yes," Li Wei continued. "Dr. Wang is most brilliant scientist. Genius inventor, comes up with all sorts of things."

Agent Hessman didn't believe that statement. Something about Dr. Wang was just off.

"Yes," Lie Wei's colleague agreed. "She very smart. She designed the temporal radiation detector the aliens seized."

"She is the only one who knows how it works," Li Wei added.

"Ah, the brains of the outfit," Claire beamed. "Maybe a few words from her, then."

Claire stepped over to the silent Dr. Wang with her mic. "Dr. Wang— or may I call you Cissy? You can call me Claire. Cissy, your fellows here brag about your brilliance, but I've always been curious how genius minds work. My husband's a genius, you know, so I definitely have an interest. Where do you get your ideas?"

Claire silently held the mic in front of Dr. Wang, who still wore a smile. Dr. Wang stared at the mic. Then she looked back at Claire without speaking.

"Oh, come on," Claire prompted. "No one is allowed to read these interviews anyway, except for all the people spying on one another. I'm just curious how the mind works. Is there some process? Maybe you take a walk in the park to think things through. Or is there some other method you use?"

Agent Hessman saw Dr. Wang's lips start to move but no words came out.

Li Wei eagerly volunteered an answer. "She says it comes to her in dreams."

"Inspirations," his colleague added. "How would you say it . . . ?"

"Epiphanies?" Claire suggested.

"Yes, epiphanies," he replied with an eager nod.

"Ah, then it's more like your subconscious is working on it," Claire said, turning the mic back to Dr. Wang.

"I, uh . . . yes," Dr. Wang replied quietly. "Epiphanies. I just see it, then make it."

"Sort of like how I hear Einstein worked things out," Claire remarked, her tone friendly. "Have you always worked like that?"

"Not always," Dr. Wang carefully admitted. "Have always been brilliant, but only after seeing reports of American time travel technology . . ."

Odd, Agent Hessman thought. *How could reports of American time travel technology trigger epiphanies?*

"What about when you were a kid," Claire pressed. "Some kids are late bloomers, others early bloomers. What was the case with you? Oh! What sort of games did you play as a child? I'm curious if they're different than what American kids would play, or if kids are the same the world over."

While Claire was passing the mic between one talkative Chinese delegate after another, Ben grinned.

Agent Hessman eyed Andros.

"Impressive," Andros admitted.

"She has confirmed that Dr. Wang is their brains," Agent Hessman stated, "and that I need to check security leaks the Chinese apparently found in our archives section that go well beyond Captain Beck."

"I'm curious about what else Dr. Wang admitted to," Mr. Thomas said, "but I don't know what to make of it."

"Neither do I," Agent Hessman agreed, "but Dr. Wang definitely merits a closer look. Andros—"

"For this we can work together," the Russian responded to the unspoken question. "I know Americans not hiding anything because you are the ones that both China and Russia steal from."

"You have a mole in our program as well?" Mr. Thomas asked with narrowed eyes.

"Of course not," the Russian said with a quiet chuckle. "We have mole in Chinese program. Just not as high up as Dr. Wang. Chinese are hard to bribe. They are more afraid of their entire families getting shot by their government if they talk."

"A policy I can sympathize with," Mr. Thomas remarked. "At least under certain circumstances."

Back with the Chinese delegation, Claire received answers to her questions from nearly everyone there. All of the delegates were quite chatty except for the reclusive Dr. Wang who seemed to have her mind on something else.

"Oh, I hope I'm not boring you with my questions, Cissy. It's just that, well, all reporters are by nature inquisitive. Of course, I guess it's that way with scientists too, just different interests. What are some of your interests outside of science?"

"My, uh . . ." Dr. Wang began, her eyes glazed and not quite focused on Claire. "I . . . have diabetes."

"Yes, I think you mentioned that," Claire replied, looking a little puzzled. "And since you brought it up, were you born with diabetes, or one of those that acquired it? Because you don't look too unhealthy."

"I stay in good... Diabetes. I have diabetes."

Agent Hessman noted Dr. Wang direct her gaze straight towards the double doors and the alien guards.

"Well," Claire said, "I guess it's time for that group picture I promised. Just one for the article. Then you can read about yourselves when your people steal it from my people."

As she dropped the mic back into her bag, she picked up the camera hanging around her neck and took a couple of steps back. The members of the Chinese delegation eagerly huddled together around Dr. Wang, all smiling and posing like eager young children. All save for Dr. Wang, who remained reticent.

"Okay everyone, smile. Say cheese. Do they even have cheese in China?"

The remark prompted the desired grins. Claire snapped one picture and then another in quick succession before thumbing the switch on the camera back to record video. She dropped the camera back into place, hanging from her neck. "I just want to thank you all for putting up with me," she said. "I know we reporters can get rather nosey."

"Our pleasure," the first Chinese delegate replied. "I can hardly wait to read the article."

At that moment, the double doors slid apart. Sonsa Tabbak stepped in, suddenly becoming the center of attention. "Apologies for the wait. Supreme Leader Kadahth and the Assembly are now ready to give you audience. Just remember this is a very distinguished body and also a place of highest security. You are being honored as diplomatic envoys from a sovereign government but remain on good behavior."

"I have vodka ready to present to your leader," Andros said. "That's about as good behavior as you can expect from country Russia."

Some of the other Russians chuckled in appreciation of their countryman's jest as they walked toward the double door. Then Chinese delegation followed, then the Americans, with Agent Hessman and Andros bringing up the rear.

As the Chinese contingent entered the long hallway, however, Dr. Wang paused to remove a syringe from her coat pocket while fixing her attention on the double doors. Fixed enough, apparently, to have forgotten Claire's presence by her side.

"If I may ask . . . ?" Claire prompted.

Dr. Wang kept her eyes on the double doors. "Insulin . . . for diabetes . . . must have insulin."

Agent Hessman's gaze snapped back to Dr. Wang, who primed her syringe.

"Funny time to worry about insulin," Claire shrugged. "We're about to meet the high muckety-muck head alien. Hey, maybe you can ask them to cure your diabetes."

Agent Hessman pursed his lips and narrowed his eyes thoughtfully.

"So, tell me, what do you plan to ask these aliens?" Claire queried the Chinese delegates as they followed the others through the doors. "How do you greet an alien ruler in the first place?"

"Dr. Wang is going to be our spokesperson," Li Wei answered. "She has a speech all ready. But I am like you. I would not know what to say to such a being."

"Cissy, you're the spokesperson?" Claire turned now back to the woman beside her. "Maybe that's why you've been holding back on your words; you're saving them up for the big event. Well, I can understand that. You must be really nervous."

Dr. Wang did not respond.

As Claire continued interviewing the Chinese nationals, Agent Hessman followed them into the hallway, his eyes focused on Dr. Wang. It was not nervousness that Agent Hessman saw in her face, however. It was more like a fixed focus on something that no one else could see. He watched as she brought the tip of her syringe up to her arm, pressed it against her skin, and held it there as they continued walking down the long hall.

"Curious," Agent Hessman quietly remarked.

"Something about Dr. Wang?" Ben asked.

"Yes." Agent Hessman turned to Dr. Weiss. "Sam, aren't diabetics supposed to inject themselves in the butt or leg or something?"

"Yes," Dr. Weiss replied.

"That's what I thought."

Agent Hessman immediately quickened his pace to catch up with Claire and Dr. Wang, who had worked their way towards the front of the line behind Sonsa Tabbak.

"Claire, don't let her use that needle!" he shouted.

"What?" Claire turned to look at Dr. Wang, who still held the needle's tip against her arm without yet injecting herself with the insulin.

"Must inject my insulin," Dr. Wang muttered.

"Cissy?" Claire prompted.

"Claire!" Agent Hessman called.

Dr. Wang suddenly shoved Claire aside and broke into a run down the hall, all the while muttering with the needle still poised against her forearm. "Must inject my insulin . . . Must inject my insulin . . ."

Claire pressed herself against the wall while Agent Hessman and Andros broke into a run down the hall and flew past her, heading for Dr. Wang.

CHAPTER TWENTY-THREE
ALIEN CHASE

"MUST INJECT MY INSULIN..."

Dr. Weiss took a more careful note of Dr. Wang's expression and actions. "The way she's been acting," he muttered, "the look on her face, the way she's talking about her insulin..."

Dr. Wang suddenly sprinted past Agent Hessman, Andros, and then Sonsa Tabbak. The two men and the alien wove their way past those ahead of them to catch up to her.

"... Must inject my insulin..."

Agent Hessman shouted, "It's a mantra. Like Samantha!"

Mr. Thomas joined Agent Hessman's pursuit.

Andros broke into a run and caught up to Dr. Wang quickly, before Agent Hessman could get to her. With one hand, Andros grabbed Dr. Wang by the shoulder and spun her around, as his other hand snatched at the syringe.

"You do not understand," Dr. Wang protested, "I must inject my insulin!" With her free hand she jabbed out a quick punch, hitting the Russian in the throat. Andros dropped immediately with a pained gurgle. She broke away chanting, "Must inject my insulin."

The other Chinese delegates had eyes only for the Russian and American pursuit of their countryman.

"American plot," one called out.

"Stop them!" shrieked another.

Sue sped past Agent Hessman and launched a sidekick into one Chinese man's midsection, tumbling him into another.

The hallway came to an abrupt end just ahead of Agent Hessman and Sue, where another two aliens dressed in brown robes stood guard. As Dr. Wang ran toward them, each guard drew out a small golden disc and aimed its shiny surface in her direction. A flash of light went off, stunning a Russian who was catching up with her and the Chinese man who was trying to pull the Russian down.

But the light had no effect on Dr. Wang.

With a loud martial cry, Dr. Wang leaped the last few yards toward the guards—farther than anyone might expect of someone her size. She landed, planting one foot into the throat of the alien on her left and a knuckle plunging hard into the forehead depression of the alien on her right. Both aliens dropped immediately.

Dr. Wang leaped to the wall on the right, her palm snapping out to press against a spot on the wall. In response, a portion of that wall slid aside. She was through the doorway in a moment—not quickly enough, however, to prevent Sue from catching up.

Sue stood in the middle of the entryway to prevent the door from closing. "This way!" she shouted.

Instead of following Sue through the door, Agent Hessman caught up with Sonsa Tabbak, who was looking around in some confusion. One of the Chinese delegates had broken away and taken out two other aliens. As the flood of Earthers poured down the hall, a team of Galnarans entered from a new set of sliding doors. They each carried golden disc weapons.

"What is happening?" Sonsa Tabbak called out. "Please stop this immediately."

"Agent Hessman, Sonsa Tabbak," Ben called.

Agent Hessman and Sonsa Tabbak turned to see Ben approaching with Claire and Dr. Weiss.

"I think you should listen to what Sam here has to say," Ben said. "He—"

"We allowed you people here as delegates to this sacred place," Sonsa Tabbak interrupted. "And this is what you do? We were going to give you a gift."

"Please, Tabbak." Dr. Weiss raised his hand and lightly tapped his cane against the floor. "Please, listen. The Chinese woman—Dr. Wang—I think she is under some sort of programmed influence and means to do harm."

"What do you mean?" Sonsa Tabbak demanded.

Dr. Weiss turned to Agent Hessman. "That woman was looking and acting just like Samantha did when those future Russians had her under their control."

"So, you think Dr. Wang is being controlled," Agent Hessman stated. "I knew something was off. But why? And by whom?"

"That, my friend, would be the question of the day," Dr. Weiss sighed.

"Lou, you've been suspicious of her all along," Claire added. "Your instincts are never wrong. But I don't think it's really her fault."

"That is ridiculous," Sonsa Tabbak replied. "You are all without weapons and anything harmful. What harm could she possibly cause?"

"I don't know," Dr. Weiss replied, "but the fact that Lou thinks there's a danger is good enough for me. Ben, you two try and stop her. Don't let me slow you down."

"Right," Ben replied as he broke into a run. "We don't need our first interstellar incident."

"And maybe I can snap some pictures of what's going on." Claire followed Ben, clutching her camera.

"Well," Dr. Weiss said, "I hope this doesn't reflect too badly on Earth as a whole."

Agent Hessman nodded his agreement and followed the others. He

THE ALIENS STEP IN

swiftly joined Sue and together, they led the pack of humans and Galnarans chasing Dr. Wang. Andros and Mr. Thomas ran right behind them, followed by the remaining Russians and Chinese. Fights broke out between humans everywhere.

Agent Hessman and Sue closed in. Dr. Wang was still a dozen feet ahead of them, coming up to an intersection of two bluish-white hallways, where two more Galnarans stood ready with golden disk weapons. Four more Galnarans joined them.

"Okay Lou," Sue asked, "what's the Reader's Digest version?"

"Dr. Wang is under some sort of control, and I'm willing to bet that—alien scans to the contrary—her insulin syringe is a lot more dangerous than it looks."

"So, if Dr. Wang wants to inject it into her arm," Sue surmised, "we can't let her. Got it!"

Sue pulled ahead of Agent Hessman, and two Galnarans raised their golden discs. Sue immediately dropped her backside to the ground, and with her feet forward, slid toward Dr. Wang. The alien weapons flashed. Both weapons hit Dr. Wang squarely, but with no effect.

Dr. Wang leaped toward the aliens with each of her feet kicking out to the side, landing squarely into the forehead of each of the two aliens. They fell to the ground.

As Dr. Wang landed with her legs spread, Sue slid between them, grabbed Dr. Wang's arms, and kicked straight up using her own momentum and Dr. Wang's legs as leverage. With a cry and a double kick straight for Sue's face, Dr. Wang brought her free hand up to block Sue's attack. She grabbed Sue's foot by the ankle and ducked to the side to avoid Sue's other foot.

Sue cried out sharply but held onto Dr. Wang's ankle.

Dr. Wang monotoned, "I must inject my insulin!"

Dr. Wang managed to bring her left foot up despite Sue's grip and stomped down hard on Sue's upper arm, releasing Sue's grip. Dr. Wang's free leg slammed a knee into Sue's raised midsection. Sue let out a hard wheeze as her other hand released its grip on Dr. Wang's other leg. Dr. Wang gave Sue one last kick before chanting, "Must inject my insulin!"

"And I must check my spleen," Sue gasped.

Agent Hessman and Andros helped Sue to her feet.

"Sue, are you alright?" Agent Hessman asked.

"She doesn't fight like a lab rat," Sue gasped on her way up. "She's stronger than she looks too."

"And with a suspiciously detailed knowledge of the layout of this place," Agent Hessman quickly noted. "We can't cut her off since we don't know the area, which means we can't let her out of our sight."

"I will catch female Chinese," Andros said, already pulling away into a run. "You rest."

"Never," Sue vowed between clenched teeth. "Pain is just weakness leaving the body, and right now I've got a lot of weakness leaving me."

Agent Hessman frowned.

"I'll be fine, Lou," Sue said. She broke into a run, though slower than before.

Behind him, Agent Hessman heard the sounds of other combat. Chinese fighting Russians, alien weapons firing down members of both delegations in paralytic spasms. Claire and Ben had managed to make it clear of the mess, as had Mr. Thomas. They joined Agent Hessman, and he pointed in the direction where Dr. Wang and Andros had run, and then led the chase anew.

☾

The hallway exited into another circular room. This one had a high domed ceiling topped by a glowing crystal ball floating near the top, glistening in different shades of blue. There was an upper balcony to one side with a partial view of an adjoining hall. At the center of the room on the floor was a sculpture of sorts, one crafted entirely of different colored lights—a hologram, though with no projectors to create it.

THE ALIENS STEP IN

Agent Hessman found Andros on the ground by the sculpture grabbing his stomach. "Female Chinese kick really hard," he gasped.

Ben and Claire came up right behind Agent Hessman.

"Are you alright?" Claire asked the Russian as she and Ben helped him to his feet.

"Dr. Wang live up to her name and kick me in the—" He offered Claire an apologetic smile. "Sorry, crude humor not for ears of pretty young woman. I'll be fine, just need drink of old Russian medicine."

"Where did Dr. Wang go?" Agent Hessman asked.

Steadying himself on his feet between the Ben and Claire, the Russian pulled out his small bottle of vodka. After a twist of the cap followed by a quick sip and a satisfied sigh, he re-secured the bottle and straightened.

"I thought you were giving that to the alien leader," Ben remarked.

"Was going to make toast together with him," Andros said with a slight shrug. "I merely take my toast early. Come, must catch woman scientist that fight like *Spetsnoz*."

"Where did Dr. Wang go?" Agent Hessman repeated.

"Black woman still after her," the Russian replied, pointing to one of three open passages connecting with the circular room.

"Are you sure you're, okay?" Ben asked.

"If black beauty can do it, so can Andros. Come!"

Agent Hessman nodded to the Russian and ran for the indicated hall.

"Hold it right there."

All heads turned to see Sonsa Tabbak enter the circular room holding a golden disc aimed in their direction. Dr. Weiss walked a pace behind Sonsa Tabbak with his cane.

"Sonsa Tabbak," Ben said, "Dr. Wang is a plant. She's up to something, and we've got to stop her."

"We have security forces that will do the job," Sonsa Tabbak replied. "The rest of the other two contingents are being gathered up, and we will soon have Dr. Wang. Our weapons will only stun, but they are still quite effective."

"I think not," Andros said. "Have already seen her take down four of your people and not slightest effect of your weapons."

"A puzzle, I admit," Sonsa Tabbak began, "but we will deal with it when we—*raaa*!" His words ended in a scream of pain as Dr. Weiss's cane came down hard to his hand—the one holding the alien weapon—and then behind his knee.

"Sorry, my friend," Dr. Weiss apologized, "but this is kind of our responsibility. Lou, go."

Agent Hessman—followed by Ben, Claire, and Andros—ran straight for the same exit as the others before them.

"Again, sorry about that," Dr. Weiss said as he jogged past Sonsa Tabbak in pursuit of his friends.

☾

Agent Hessman caught up to Sue as Dr. Wang fought off three more aliens in brown robes, none of whose stun weapons seemed to affect her. The corridor they walked along curved widely with no visible exits or other hallways that Agent Hessman could see— but he had come to learn that meant nothing around here.

Sue put up her hand. "Stop, Lou. Watch." She narrowed her eyes and studied the way the doctor fought as she faced off against the aliens.

The aliens were taller than Dr. Wang, and while one of them appeared to have some physical combat skill, they seemed more reliant on their technology and, Agent Hessman guessed, whatever psychic aptitude they may have possessed. But Dr. Wang appeared immune. She already had one of them on the ground unconscious and was giving a leaping kick to another one, aiming directly for the depression at the center of the forehead.

"Knows right where to aim," Sue remarked. "And from the looks of it, she has a black belt in at least three different styles that I know of. Plus, I can personally testify to her strength. A bit more than what a high-class bookworm would have time to master."

A second alien was felled, leaving only one.

"Our girl there is no scientist," Sue remarked to Agent Hessman.

"Except that when Claire was interviewing them all, the rest of the Chinese representatives vouched for her as their number one genius," Agent Hessman countered.

"And why," a huffing Mr. Thomas spat out as he caught up with them, "would the Chinese send their best scientist on such a risky mission? Especially with the risk of an alien interrogation?"

"One of several very good questions," Agent Hessman agreed. "Sue, care to get the answers?"

"Round two, coming up," she stated.

The third alien fell just as Sue came up behind Dr. Wang. Dr. Wang spun around quickly, her arms already up in a block. Sue leaped at her with a helicopter kick. Spinning legs met against two upraised arms and a sturdy stance. As Sue made contact, her kick turned into a fall, then a roll, quickly bringing her back to her feet. She faced off once again against Dr. Wang.

"I must inject my insulin," Dr. Wang insisted.

"Yeah, heard it before," Sue replied as she slipped into a battle crouch. "Which is why it's not happening. Now hand over the syringe."

With her gaze fixed on Sue, Dr. Wang raised the syringe high in her right hand and positioning the needle over her left arm. Sue lunged, grabbing for Dr Wang's syringe hand and at the same time, struggling to pull it away from Wang's left arm.

"Must . . . inject self," Dr. Wang chanted, struggling against Sue.

"Find something new to say," Sue replied between clenched teeth.

"Cossack to the rescue!"

Andros charged into Dr. Wang's other side, grabbing her left arm to pull it away from the one holding the needle. An effort that, with his greater weight and Sue's assistance, should have been a lot easier than it turned out to be. Muscles bulged on Dr. Wang's arms as she struggled.

"Dr. Wang, we are here to help you!"

A wild cry arose from the remaining members of the Chinese delegation at the opposite end of the hall. They were heading straight for the struggle. Behind them, one Russian gave chase, followed by an alien who was attempting to aim his golden disk weapon at all of them from around the curvature of the hallway.

Sue and Andros were each tackled by a Chinese combatant, leaving Dr. Wang to wiggle free.

"I must inject my insulin." The doctor stepped free of her compatriots who were rolling around on the floor.

The fight against these other two took less effort than the struggle with Dr. Wang. A kick to the groin and elbow punch to the side of the head, and Sue's opponent was down, while Andros grabbed his opponent in a bear hug until the struggling gradually diminished. It was enough time, though, for Dr. Wang to begin her escape. Agent Hessman charged Dr. Wang, but she met his attack with a swift kick to the throat with her superhuman strength, and he went down.

A Russian blocked her escape.

Dr. Wang met him with a puzzled look. "I must inject my insulin," she said in an almost sorrowful tone. She leaped into the air just as the Russian charged her, and her foot snapped out with a sharp kick directly into his face. The man dropped as she landed.

"Cissy!" Claire cried, approaching the woman with Ben. Dr. Weiss followed a small distance behind them. The men paused as Claire ran toward Dr. Wang. Andros and Sue dropped their own now-unconscious opponents to stand ready for anything.

"Cissy, wait!"

Dr. Wang paused with a curious look on her face as the reporter closed in.

"Reporter Claire," Andros warned. "Stay away. Female Chinese is killer."

"She's far more than she appears, Claire," Sue warned.

But Claire, as usual, approached her subject with determination.

Agent Hessman stood ready to assist, knowing enough to stay out of

Claire's way. She would get information. She always did. The rest of the team held back too, though in Ben's case it was with a particularly pained expression.

When Claire got within a dozen feet, Dr. Wang quickly brought the needle of the injector up to the side of her neck.

Claire immediately stopped in her tracks.

"I must inject my insulin."

"I understand," Claire said calmly, opening her hands to reveal empty palms. "But you don't really want to hurt anyone, do you? You're a scientist, your goal is to learn new things. Right?"

"I need . . . to inject my insulin. I must inject—"

"Insulin's really important for a diabetic," Claire calmly agreed, "but how long have you been a diabetic? My readers will want to know."

"I . . . I . . . not sure. Must inject myself."

Andros, apparently growing impatient, began sneaking toward Dr. Wang. Agent Hessman scowled, hoping to deter him, but Andros kept creeping toward the doctor.

"You know," Claire continued, "I have a friend named Samantha. At one point, some bad people did something to her much like what we think someone did to you. She'd been programmed to do something she didn't want to. Did someone program you, Cissy? Who was it?"

For a moment Dr. Wang paused, hand shaking. Then the faint creek of a shoe snapped her attention toward Andros, who was closing in.

"No! I must inject!" Dr. Wang's leg snapped out to catch Andros by the shin. She spun away and ran down the hall leaving Claire in her wake. "Must inject! Must inject!"

Sue didn't waste a moment and gave chase.

"Don't just stand there," shouted Mr. Thomas. "Everyone after her before we find out the hard way what's really in that syringe!"

The chase resumed, though how they would stop her once they caught up to her, no one knew.

CHAPTER TWENTY-FOUR
BOMB!

THE OTHER END OF THE curved hall brought them back to a familiar looking intersection—the same one where Dr. Wang had dropped the first two Galnarans. They had been dragged to one side where an alien medic was tending them. A small mixed group of Chinese and Russian delegates stood frozen in place while Galnaran security guards secured them.

This time, however, Dr. Wang took a different exit. "I must inject myself! Must inject..."

Dr. Wang bolted down the hallway with Sue right behind her, Andros a close second, and Agent Hessman bringing up third in a heated race to an unknown destination.

They charged through a large open archway and emerged in a mammoth chamber.

Agent Hessman thought it resembled a gigantic amphitheater. The diameter stretched a thousand feet with walls and floor of a familiar bluish-white. High above, the domed ceiling was solid navy blue. The first row of raised seats was located behind a ten-foot wall. They continued for five rows, most of which were filled with Galnarans and a scattering of other

unfamiliar alien races.

Directly opposite the entrance, the rows converged with a large box seat, much like an emperor of old Rome might have occupied. Glittering jewels of red, blue, and bright green gilded the box. The box itself seemed to be constructed from something similar to white marble. Dozens of Galnarans sat there. In the center, the most ornate seat held a being who was obviously Supreme Leader Kadahth.

The second after the delegations came running in, a voice boomed loudly across the amphitheater from an invisible sound system. "Announcing the delegation from Earth here to seek audience before Supreme Leader Kadahth."

Dr. Wang fixated on the Galnaran in that notable central seat and ran toward him.

"Must inject. Must inject."

"Dr. Wang, you've got to stop," Agent Hessman hollered.

Dr. Wang glanced at him. "No! I must inject myself before the leader."

Agent Hessman stopped. *Before the leader?* That last part of her statement was new.

The amphitheater audience looked down upon the events curiously. No one made a move to intervene. Agent Hessman suspected they found it amusing or entertaining but nothing to be concerned with. After all, the Earthers had been disarmed before coming in.

The reason behind their lack of concern became obvious when several Galnaran guards emerged from other points around the amphitheater and aimed their golden discs out at the arguing Earthers before them.

Dr. Wang paused at the sight, giving the others a chance to catch up. Andros lowered his head as if he were a charging rhinoceros, and Sue pressed her aching body to its limits. Agent Agent Hessman passed both of the wounded warriors and leaped through the air at Dr. Wang. Behind him, Mr. Thomas was doing his best to catch up.

An explosion of golden rays flashed out while Agent Hessman was still in the air. The blast hit Dr. Wang, Sue, Andros, and Mr. Thomas. Dr. Wang,

THE ALIENS STEP IN

as before, seemed unphased. The other three immediately froze and tumbled down in their tracks, completely paralyzed. Sue landed onto her face with a crash, rolling over until she was on her back with limbs in the air, frozen in mid-motion. Mr. Thomas lay on his side against the hard plastic-like floor, while Andros ended up face-down.

Agent Hessman landed on top of Dr. Wang with his arms wrapped around her.

As he did, Dr. Wang shouted, "No, I must inject myself. You must not stop me."

They rolled across the ground, Dr. Wang trying to break free.

Times like this, Agent Hessman thought, *I wish I didn't have a code against hitting a woman. That's what Sue is for.*

As Dr. Wang pressed against his body, displaying far more strength than her small body should hold, Agent Hessman broke his hold in favor of a desperate grab for her syringe. They struggled, each trying to get tug the needle free.

The Galnaran audience murmured their confusion.

"What are they fighting over?"

"Security scans showed it to be a simple medical injector. Harmless."

"Why all the fuss?"

"Is this some strange Earth ritual?"

"You must not take my injector," Dr. Wang said harshly into Agent Hessman's face. "I need my injection. I must have my injection."

Each time Dr. Wang brought the needle closer to her own arm or neck, Agent Hessman pulled it away. Limbs shook in the contest, all muscles tensed. Pound for pound in a straight-on wrestling match, they were more evenly matched than Agent Hessman wanted to admit.

"Must . . . inject . . ."

Claire and Ben charged into the amphitheater and stopped short.

Sue could still not move, but she could still talk, and she did so. Loudly. "Claire! Get that needle!"

"And someone move me from face into ground," Andros added from his frozen position.

Claire reached into her shoulder bag for her mic. Ben placed a restraining hand on her shoulder.

"I'm just going in for distraction." Claire shrugged.

"Then I'm your backup," Ben replied.

Claire ran directly toward Agent Hessman and Dr. Wang, while Ben circled around behind them.

☾

As Claire and Ben pursued Dr. Wang, Dr. Weiss entered the large archway accompanied by Sonsa Tabbak, Tahsa Ray'ahl, and two other Galnarans.

Dr. Weiss spoke amiably with the alien group. "We've run into it once before," he said. "Dr. Wang is showing all the signs. She's been programmed, all right, and Lou was simply trying to stop whatever she's up to. Everyone else from the American and Russian delegations followed his lead. The Chinese, I imagine, were simply trying to defend their countryman in what they thought was some nefarious plot. But no plot, I assure you, except for whatever Dr. Wang is trying to accomplish."

"Even if that may be true," Tahsa Ray'ahl insisted, "there is no harm that she can do to anyone here. That is a simple medical injector, and scans confirmed it is filled only with normal insulin."

"Ah, but that is what set Agent Hessman off," Dr. Weiss beamed. "Very observant on his part, I'll admit, but insulin is injected in the thigh, not in the arm. Diabetics are rather particular about where they're injected."

"I see what you mean," Sonsa Tabbak mused. "But then to what purpose? What harm could simple insulin wreak?"

"That, my alien friends, is for you people to figure out, I'm afraid. Oh, and sorry about the smack with the cane, but by the time you would have listened to me, Dr. Wang would have accomplished her mission, whatever that is."

"I quite understand."

Sonsa Tabbak gave Dr. Weiss's words some thought as the struggle continued in the middle of the amphitheater with Claire trying her own careful approach. The alien needed only a moment to make his decision.

"Turn off the paralysis fields on the Earthers," he ordered. "And perform a much deeper scan of Dr. Wang. Full spectrum."

One of the Galnarans replied with a nod and tapped some sort of wrist controller. A light briefly flickered around Sue, Andros, and Mr. Thomas, and they began to move once more. Then a spotlight shown down from high above, centered on Dr. Wang—the deeper scan that Sonsa Tabbak had ordered. The sight drew closer attention from the circle of observing aliens, in particular, from Supreme Leader Kadahth.

"Ow," Andros said as he rolled over onto his back, "I think I broke my nose."

"You're Russian," Sue quipped, "you'll make it work."

"Ha, that I will."

As Andros sat up, a sudden look of concern slid across his face. He quickly ran his hands through his pockets until he brought out the bottle of vodka. A look of relief swept over him. "Ah, still intact. Would not forgive self if contents of gift wasted on floor."

Sue rolled her eyes at the sentiment and leaped up to her feet, while Mr. Thomas climbed more gradually to his.

☾

"Must inject myself! Give me my injector. Please!"

Dr. Wang and Hessman were still pulling at the other, wrestling for control of the syringe. Agent Hessman managed a more careful look into Dr. Wang's eyes. She was pleading, and yet behind that beseeching look, her eyes held a suggestion of confusion as if she wasn't entirely certain of her own actions but needed to do them anyway.

"Dr. Wang," he said, "you have been programmed by someone, and whatever you think you want to do, it's not you deciding to do it."

Dr. Wang's eyes fogged over for a moment, then resumed their fixed look, her actions more insistent than before. "My syringe. You must let me have it. You must let me inject myself!"

"Sorry, but I've a feeling that would be a very bad idea."

Dr. Wang cried out as she powered her way to her feet, dragging Agent Hessman right along with her and refusing to let go. By degrees, the syringe came closer to her chest, then with equally slow degrees, back towards Agent Hessman. And all the while the spotlight continued to track Dr. Wang.

"Excuse me Dr. Wang, but I need a few more questions for my readers."

Dr. Wang and Agent Hessman turned toward the voice. Claire stood a few feet to Dr. Wang's left with her mic held out at arm's length, a hopeful smile on her face.

As Dr. Wang's head turned to the left, Ben came upon her right side and wrapped his arms around her body, pinning her arms to her side.

"No! You must not stop me!"

"Sorry," Ben apologized. "I'm not really the physical type, but we'd like a closer look at that syringe."

Dr. Wang screamed, then stomped a foot down hard onto Ben's left instep. She slammed a knee into Agent Hessman's groin and leaped backward, victoriously waving her syringe.

"My insulin. I must inject it now."

"Not on my money!" Sue came at Dr. Wang in a flying tackle, slamming full into her midsection and tumbling them both to the ground. Dr. Wang stretched the arm holding the syringe high and away, and Sue reached after it. Inches away, but now on the ground where weight mattered more, Sue had the advantage. Even so, all Dr. Wang needed to do was get the needle near her body—any part of her body.

As Dr. Wang attempted to turn the syringe around in her hand for better aim toward her other arm, a booted foot came down onto her forearm, holding it firm—a boot owned by one terse-looking man. Mr. Thomas.

"Were we on my home turf," Mr. Thomas flatly stated, "I would have shot you first and then begun the investigation."

The spotlight on Dr. Wang snapped off, replaced by a larger floodlight encompassing the entire group.

A firm voice of authority rang out loudly: "Stop this immediately!"

The voice echoed out from the seat of the supreme leader as its occupant rose to his feet. All fighting stopped as a wide circle of guards, armed now with something longer and more pointed than simple golden discs, surrounded the combatants.

Sue pushed herself off Dr. Wang with her hands raised. The others followed suit. Mr. Thomas stepped away from Dr. Wang, who got back to her feet.

Supreme Leader Kadahth stood before them. Slightly taller than other Galnarans, he wore a gold jumpsuit, his black cape covered with star speckles and silver trim.

Mr. Thomas glanced sideways at Agent Hessman, who took his cue and stepped forward to speak. He was not allowed the chance, however.

Dr. Wang verbally raced to make her case. "Please, I simply need to take my insulin. I beg of you, Qual Ahk-Sonsa Kadahth, Supreme Leader of the Interstellar Union, to let me take my injection. I need my insulin."

"A simple medical need," Supreme Leader Kadahth stated. "What can be so wrong with that?"

Looking hopeful, Dr. Wang aimed the syringe at her left arm, but she was suddenly grabbed by the wrists. Both wrists, actually. Sue held the right wrist and Andros the left.

"I suspect it is not so simple a matter." Agent Hessman stepped around them and presented himself to Supreme Leader Kadahth with a slight bow of his head. "My name is Special Agent Lou Hessman, and my job is to know when people are up to something they shouldn't be. Dr. Wang here is not what she seems, no matter what your scans may say. And while I don't know what could be so dangerous about a simple insulin syringe, I am certain that there is a danger."

#16 – Qual Ahk-Sonsa Kadahth
SUPREME LEADER OF THE INTERSTELLAR UNION

"Be that as it may, Special Agent Hessman," Supreme Leader Kadahth stated, "we have every confidence in our own abilities to detect any danger before it happens."

The light surrounding the whole group now switched off. An announcement flooded the room: "Attention! Preliminary deep scans suggest that Earther Dr. Cissy Wang has been conditioned with subconscious programming technology that is well beyond anything available on Earth."

Dr. Wang's right foot slammed down hard onto Sue's. Her right elbow crashed into Sue's rib cage, while her left elbow slammed into Andros's side. Their holds broken, she leaped away and quickly stabbed the needle into her arm.

"Finally," she sighed.

Sue came in with a tackle a moment too late, and Andros dove at Dr. Wang's feet. But this time Dr. Wang didn't struggle. The injector dropped from her grip and her face lost all expression. In the moment it took Sue and Andros to take her down, Dr. Wang's body was already growing pale, her face devoid of expression. She muttered a few words, but they were unknown to anyone else from earth.

Agent Hessman suspected the words were known to Sonsa Tabbak, though, as the alien cast a quizzical look at their utterance.

Dr. Wang began to spasm and glow slightly. Sue and Andros pulled away.

Agent Hessman shouted loud and clear, "I know a bomb when I see one. Everyone, run for it!"

Sue and Andros bolted away following Ben and Claire, who were already making good distance across the amphitheater floor.

Agent Hessman and Agent Thomas hit heels to the floor.

As Dr. Wang continued to spasm and utter alien words, the glow from within her body grew. The alien audience finally realized this was far more than some internal Earther feud and started to their feet, several looking for ways out. Panic rose as Dr. Wang's convulsions continued to worsen.

Still back near the large arched entry, Dr. Weiss began backing away too.

Sonsa Tabbak stood firm and shouted an order. "Secure Dr. Wang. Level one forcefield. Now. Complete enclosure."

Ha, Agent Hessman thought. The alien had been paying attention to everything Dr. Weiss told him. Now, finally, he realized the danger.

Immediately, a glittering dome of light enveloped Dr. Wang's body from head to toe. Her body grew brighter until it looked like her skin was lit from within, her eyes gleaming orbs—and then it happened. Dr. Wang transformed into an explosive mass of energy, filling the forcefield containing her with a brilliance to rival the twin stars of Setra. It held for several long, breathtaking seconds.

From the Galnaran audience in the high seats to the Earthers trapped so close to the source below, no one moved. Not a breath was taken. All knew that if the containment field ever found its limit, there would be no place far enough away to run and escape the blast.

Eventually, the brilliance dimmed. It became clear that no sign of Dr. Wang's body remained, just the glow of a small stellar ember within the containment field.

Held breaths were released, sighs given all around, even from amongst some of the aliens present. Agent Hessman unclenched his fists and checked his team. Claire clung to Ben, Dr. Weiss stepped out from behind Sonsa Tabbak, and Andros was doubly relieved once he confirmed that his bottle of vodka was still secured. Up in the main booth, Supreme Leader Kadahtt leaned calmly back in his chair, making of himself a living example of tranquility for everyone else.

"Dispose the containment sphere," Sonsa Tabbak ordered.

At his command, the still-glowing capsule of force floated up towards the ceiling high above, where a panel slid aside to permit it through.

Agent Hessman dusted himself off quickly paced across the open floor back to Sonsa Tabbak. "Might I make a suggestion?" he asked.

"I need not telepathy to know what that will be," Sonsa Tabbak replied, then addressed the guards. "Get all the other Earthers in here. Put them all through a thorough deep scan."

As the guards left to be gather the remaining Chinese and Russian representatives, Sonsa Tabbak glanced at Dr. Weiss by his side. "Even you, my new friend."

"Oh, quite understood," Dr. Weiss agreed. "As I said, we've been through this sort of thing once before."

As aliens scurried about to fulfill their orders, Agent Hessman could not help but find his thoughts lingering. If not for a slightly different set of circumstances, the glowing ember that was all that remained of Dr. Wang could have been Samantha.

Maybe the love between them had made the difference after all.

CHAPTER TWENTY-FIVE
AUDIENCE

EVERYONE NOW GATHERED AT ONE end of the sunken amphitheater floor: Agent Hessman's team, the Russian team, and the remains of the Chinese team. Twenty of Sonsa Tabbak's people, all well-armed, surrounded the middle of the amphitheater floor. A couple of suspicious looking, gun-like projections suspended from the high ceiling were aimed at the group of Earthers. One by one, each human was forced to stand under a beam of light for a thorough scan.

Meanwhile, the aliens seated in the stadium above and around them retook their seats, following the example of their Supreme Leader who remained calmly in his own ornate chair awaiting the scan results.

A few Galnarans huddled in conference with Sonsa Tabbak out of hearing range of the Earthers. Not that it mattered. For that conference, the telepathic translation field they had been enjoying the benefits of had apparently been turned off. All Agent Hessman and the others could see were Sonsa Tabbak and his staffers simply staring at one another with an occasional alien word exchanged.

Naturally, the remainder of the Chinese team were the first to undergo

THE ALIENS STEP IN

the deep scan.

"This shouldn't hurt any more than their tunnel scanner," Dr. Weiss remarked to Agent Hessman. "The only difference is how deep it goes. After what we saw, I expect they'll be scanning us down to our cellular structure."

"And exactly how strict do you think they'll be with what they consider dangerous?" Claire asked.

"Were I them," Mr. Thomas replied, "I would disintegrate anyone with anything that appeared the least suspicious."

"I see," Claire said with a slightly nervous swallow. "So then if you had someone that, oh say, had a metabolism or something that was maybe about a century out of step with anyone else . . ."

Mr. Thomas did not reply.

Claire cast a nervous glance at her husband. Ben wrapped an arm around her and pulled her tight into her side, whispering reassurances into her ear as he nuzzled her. "Don't worry, they're only looking for security threats. They already know about your origins, remember."

"Just so long as they don't try to temporally correct me away from you."

"I would object most strenuously if they tried," Ben assured her.

One by one, each individual was marched up to the scan location where they were forced to stand for at least a minute as a beam of light fell upon them. Upon completion of the scan, they were led away to another section of the floor where they waited under guard for results.

The first of the Chinese, it seemed to Agent Hessman, looked exceptionally nervous. As if he expected he might blow up just like Dr. Wang or something similar if he stepped into the light. One of the alien guards motioned with his disc-like weapon as though it were a frisbee. That solved the man's hesitation. That and a few words from the same guard: "You do not have to be conscious to go through the scan."

The man quickly stepped into the light. Soon, he was followed by the rest of his group.

Once the Chinese were finished, the Russians came. The first to step under the light was Andros Kortnev.

"I hope I am not secret bomb like Chinese doctor woman," he quipped as he stepped forward. "For then I would not have chance to drink toast with Supreme Leader."

"Rest assured, that bottle of alcoholic beverage on your person will be scanned just as thoroughly as yourself," an alien guard told Andros as the light came down upon him.

"Good! Then you will know what good Russian vodka is supposed to be, not the cheap stuff we allow to export to western nations."

As the Russian waited within the bath of light, Ben drew closer to Dr. Weiss and Agent Hessman for a quick conference. "Sam," he began, "what do you make of any of this? How could Dr. Wang have exploded like that?"

"It's beyond me," Dr. Weiss shrugged. "Something to do with her insulin is all I know. Assuming it *was* insulin, of course. Lou, any thoughts?"

"I know only that she was obviously a lot more insistent about that injection than a diabetic would be, given the circumstances," Agent Hessman replied. "How it did what it did was not nearly as important to me at the time as the fact that it was supposed to do something. The technical details are not for me to figure out, but Dr. Wang was apparently part of some plot that involved the elimination of this place."

"What if you had to guess?" Ben prompted.

"If I had to guess?" Agent Hessman mused for a moment. "If I had to guess, Dr. Wang's living bomb was meant for the alien Supreme Leader. An assassination attempt."

"By Chinese spies?" Claire interjected. "How could they even know about the aliens or their leaders, much less want to kill any of them?"

"Not the Chinese," Dr. Weiss said with a shake of his head. "Turning someone into a living bomb with that much power is as beyond anyone on Earth as that handheld temporal gizmo of the Chinese team."

Something for them to consider as they watched the other members of the Russian team gradually led through the light. When it finally came time for the American team to be scanned, Sue was the first to step forward. There was not a bit of hesitation in her step as she went into the beam of light. She simply fixed the alien monitoring her with a glare and waited. When the alien finally motioned her away to join the others who had been scanned, Andros raised a little cheer.

"*Ura!* Favorite American woman not be bomb. Except maybe *da* bomb. Now maybe we can go on date?"

Sue approached with an even look, returning his smile with a level stare before replying. "When this mission is completed, if you can best me in a fair fight two out of three times, I'll consent to that date. Beat me just once out of three and you've earned a kiss but no date."

"Ah, then there is hope. Russians have waged war for less chances than that. But what if I beat you all three times?"

"It won't happen."

"But if it does?" he pressed, taking a step closer.

"A big if," she replied, "but if you do manage that feat, then . . . I might entertain a marriage proposal."

"*Ura!* I will train like *Spetsnoz* to win that chance."

Dr. Weiss stepped into the scanner beam next, and when he finally came through to the other side, Sonsa Tabbak stepped over for a brief word. "I am glad to see that you are not like Dr. Cissy Wang," the alien told him. "For now, we can be friends."

"Not nearly as glad as I am," Dr. Weiss replied. "I'd hate to find out that my favorite cane was a bomb or something."

"Our scans confirmed that you are perfectly fine, and in fact that you do not need that cane to walk with at all."

"Yeah, I know," Dr. Weiss confessed. "I fully recovered a little while back."

"Then why do you use it?"

To the alien's question, Dr. Weiss replied with a twinkle in his eye as leaned closer. "It's all about the look, my friend. It lends an air of dignity and respect. A small portion of something I think we Earthers have that we can teach you people of Galnar."

"Oh?" Sonsa Tabbak's large, flanged ears twitched once with curiosity as he asked his next question. "And what is it that your species has that you could possibly teach us?"

"A little thing we call social graces. With all due respect, from what I've seen you are a bit lacking in that department."

The alien regarded him first curiously. Then his mouth widened into a smile, and the whiskers on his nose twitched a little. He replied with a slight bow of his head. "I concede the point, Dr. Weiss. Perhaps there is something of your social graces that you can teach me."

"Then your first lesson is that you address friends by their first names."

"As you wish. Sam. Now if you would kindly join the others so we can finish this procedure."

Dr. Weiss replied with a slight nod of his own and joined the others who had been through the scanner.

Mr. Thomas was next, stepping unafraid into the light, meeting his alien examiner with a look of equal intensity to the light before being permitted to step away.

"That is a worrisome looking human," the Galnaran guard remarked of the man.

Then it came Claire's turn.

"Don't worry," Ben said to her frowning face, "you'll do fine."

"Oh, it's not that," she replied. "I just realized that I don't have a souvenir from this place yet. Think they might give me some alien watch-bob or something?"

Under the direction of an alien guard, Claire stepped into the scanner beam then waited. A minute later she was motioned out of the beam, but she was not permitted to join the others. One of the observing aliens took her aside for a brief chat.

"What's wrong?" she immediately asked. "Am I a bomb? Or is there a problem because I'm not originally from this time?"

"No problem with that, Mrs. Hill-Stein," the alien replied. "You have left no temporal anomalies behind you and present no security dangers to us."

"Then what?"

"Merely a small item that the deep scan has picked up which I thought you should be aware of."

"An anomaly?"

Ben and Agent Hessman strained to hear what the alien said next, but its voice lowered. Then Claire suddenly jumped up on her tiptoes and flung her arms around the alien for a tight hug before breaking away to join the others.

"Now what do you figure that was about?" Ben pondered.

"Some sort of good news, apparently, but beyond that I couldn't say what," Agent Hessman shrugged. "Okay, you're next."

When Ben stepped into the beam, a grinning Claire joined with the other scanned Earthers. Before Claire uttered a word about her experience, Sue greeted her with a smile and a warm hug and whispered words of congratulations in her ear.

Agent Hessman frowned, puzzled.

Ben watched Claire and Sue with a curious gaze. Once he was cleared by the scanner, he approached Claire. "What did the alien tell you?"

"Oh, nothing . . ." she said, suppressing a giggle. "Much."

"Should I be worried? Does it concern me?"

"No, and yes."

Sue rolled her eyes but remained silent.

"Then what?" Ben asked.

"Oh . . . you'll be finding out in a few months."

Agent Hessman smiled when he heard that, but Ben still looked puzzled.

Then it was Agent Hessman's turn to step into the light. After a clipped step into the beam and standing in silence until the beam clicked off, he was motioned to join his fellow Earthers while the Galnaran technician reported the results to Sonsa Tabbak.

"They have all been cleared, Sonsa," said the technician. "No further signs of any contamination."

"That is good," Sonsa Tabbak replied.

A raised right hand from Sonsa Tabbak and twenty of the guards left, leaving only a small contingent that might be expected when such a group of foreign dignitaries visited their Supreme Leader for the first time. The Galnaran walked over to the group of humans, several of them chatting amongst their own about the recent events, save for Ben wondering about something else.

"A few months? Now what in the world could you mean? And why are you grinning so much?" he said to Claire.

"Since it is I who must win the fights," Andros said to Sue, "then I will choose the location of each contest."

"Acceptable," Sue replied. "But that's assuming it doesn't conflict with my duties or schedule. Where would our first fight be?"

"How does Hawaii sound? I hear it is good place to wrestle."

While Sue fenced with the Russian's suggestive quips, one of the Chinese approached Mr. Thomas and Agent Hessman. "We had no idea Dr. Wang was . . . a bomb. We are as in the dark as you are."

"Of course," Mr. Thomas snapped back. "You just wanted to undermine the temporal integrity of our nation, is all."

To which the other had no reply.

"A few months," Ben said. "Now what could . . ."

"You have all been cleared," Sonsa Tabbak announced.

"Good," Mr. Thomas said briskly. "Then perhaps you could enlighten us as to exactly what's been going on. What was in that syringe besides insulin?"

"The syringe was not at fault," Sonsa Tabbak explained. "It was indeed simply insulin. However, Dr. Wang's body had apparently been integrated with various substances that, while harmless in themselves, when combined with insulin become a very effective explosive."

"Ah, I get it," Dr. Weiss spoke up. "That's just like how on Earth you can combine various everyday detergent ingredients to create nerve gas."

"Exactly," Sonsa Tabbak agreed. "Nothing that in themselves would have alerted our security scanners. Initially, everything appeared normal for a human of Earth, but the later deeper scans have since revealed several anomalies about Dr. Cissy Wang."

"She wasn't human?" Dr. Weiss asked.

"No, she was quite human," Sonsa Tabbak corrected. "The changes our later scans revealed were installed at some point after her birth. Either she had been taken away as a child to be altered and programmed, or the job was done right there on Earth by an alien agent. In either case, the result is what you saw."

"Question for our Chinese companions," Agent Hessman stated. "Was Dr. Wang on the team that developed the technology behind that handheld temporal gizmo of yours?"

The same one of the Chinese team that had apologized earlier now replied with a nod.

"It was Dr. Wang who developed everything," he replied. "We could not have made such advances without her."

"Then that was how the advanced alien time travel technology was introduced," Sonsa Tabbak concluded. "An alien power used Dr. Wang to feed the technology to her countrymen under the guise of being her own inventions."

"That's it," Dr. Weiss remarked. "There's no other way of explaining how advanced that device looked. I knew there was no way anyone on Earth could have designed that thing. But why would any of your people want to help the Chinese like that?"

"A few months..." Ben was still muttering to himself.

Claire and Sue exchanged smirks.

"For that answer, I will let our Supreme Leader explain everything himself," Sons Tabbak said to Dr. Weiss. "Stay here until I bid you to approach."

With a faint nod, he crossed the amphitheater to the large dais where the alien leader sat in his booth a dozen feet above floor level. They conversed in a combination of their alien language and moments of silence that Agent Hessman guessed to be something more telepathic. During this conference, Sonsa Tabbak handed the Chinese temporal radiation detector over to his leader, who examined it as they communicated.

"A few months..." Ben continued to ponder. "And the way you're looking ready to burst like that you'd think—"

Then he stopped, eyes growing wide. Slowly he turned to face his wife with a look of shock. No words were said. He just stared directly into her eyes. Claire replied with a simple but rapid nod, her eyes beaming. Ben's shock then evolved very quickly into joy. He flung his arms around Claire and lifted her up from the ground for a loving hug—which she quite eagerly returned.

He finally caught on, Agent Hessman thought.

"Now what, if I may ask, is going on there?" Dr. Weiss wondered.

"Men," Sue said with a roll of her eyes. "You're about as quick to pick up on body language as a blind man. Don't worry Sam, I imagine it'll be clear in about nine months."

"Nine... oh. I see." Dr. Weiss grinned.

By the time Ben let Claire's feet touch the ground again, Sonsa Tabbak had finished his conversation with the alien leader and returned to the human contingent.

"The delegations from Earth may now step forward to speak with Qual Ahk-Sonsa Kadahth," Sonsa Tabbak announced.

Mr. Thomas was first to respond, stepping out in front of the rest and setting a confident pace behind Sonsa Tabbak. Agent Hessman followed, then Dr. Weiss, Sue with Andros, and behind them, Claire and Ben, arm in arm. After the American team came the Russians. The Chinese contingent staying towards the rear, their heads hanging with collective guilty looks.

As they crossed the vast amphitheater floor, the audience of aliens quieted down in anticipation of the dignity of the upcoming encounter. When they were within a few yards of the wall beneath the leader's booth, Sonsa Tabbak brought them to a halt with a raised hand.

"Humans of Earth, may I present our Supreme Leader, Qual Ahk-Sonsa Kadahth."

Agent Hessman stepped up beside Mr. Thomas, and the two bowed their heads respectfully. The others followed suit, though Ben remained holding onto Claire while doing so.

Mr. Thomas spoke first. "Supreme Leader Kadahth, my name is Mr. Rutger Thomas, direct representative of the President of the United States of America."

"Yes, we have been informed of all your identities."

The Supreme Leader spoke in a voice a little deeper than Sonsa Tabbak's, his tone even, not patronizing but still making his point clear enough. Mr. Thomas bit his lip as Supreme Leader Kadahth continued.

"You represent a leader of your world but are not the leader of this group. That, I believe, is Special Agent Lou Hessman."

Mr. Thomas fell back into studied silence, and Agent Hessman stepped forward with a nod.

Andros stepped up beside Agent Hessman. "Andros Kortnev, leader of the Russian group," he said.

"Our leader was Dr. Cissy Wang," said one of the Chinese delegates.

"Then you will remain silent and listen." Supreme Leader Kadahth spoke with an even and non-condescending tone. "Your Dr. Cissy Wang made her point clear enough earlier."

The Chinese delegate nodded and slipped into silence, content to let the rest have the floor and perhaps eager to have their role in events forgotten.

"I know your questions," Supreme Leader Kadahth stated. "First, let me say that none of my people helped the Chinese to try and destroy your world."

"Then who?" Andros asked.

"Other aliens," Agent Hessman realized. "Just like we have other nations."

"Quite right, Agent Hessman," Supreme Leader Kadahth replied. "I represent the Interstellar Union based here on Galnar. As you have guessed, however, ours is not the only governmental body in this galaxy. There are others, and not all of them are friendly. You heard the words Dr. Cissy Wang spoke?"

"Yes," Agent Hessman replied, "but in no language I recognized."

"Nor I," Dr. Weiss replied behind him.

"That is because they were spoken in the language of Katan," the Supreme Leader explained. "They come from a world named Baroka-Zet of the Trappis Cluster Alliance, and they are ones with whom we are having what you would call a 'cold war.' Your Dr. Wang was being used by the Katan."

"But why?" Andros asked. "What could we have that advanced creatures would not have better?"

"I would think that obvious," Agent Hessman stated. "It's not what we have, but where we are."

"Strategic location," Andros said as the light dawned on his face. "Ever the bane of primitive peoples in wake of advancing armies."

"Correct," the Supreme Leader replied. "Using Dr. Wang was the perfect way for the Katan to meet their goals without allowing their hand to be detected until it was too late. Their plan was nearly perfect and would have worked if not for the reasoning skills and human—"

He broke off for a moment, exchanging a brief alien word with Sonsa Tabbak, who replied with, "Gut instinct."

"Yes," Supreme Leader Kadahth continued. "If not for Agent Hessman's reasoning skills and human gut instinct. For that, we commend and thank you."

"I am honored," Agent Hessman replied. "But what exactly *was* their goal?"

"It is as you have said," the Supreme Leader continued, his words carrying across the entire amphitheater. "They wished to gain a strategic advantage in their game against the Interstellar Union, the result of which would have wiped out your entire world. You see, we had detected Earth's time travel experiments. That is why we had a vessel there in the first place. Sonsa Tabbak had been assigned to watch over your progress and make sure

THE ALIENS STEP IN

that nothing got out of control. If something occurred which your people could handle, then his presence would have never been revealed. Only in an emergency would he be allowed to interfere."

"Such as the temporal cascade effect that we nearly witnessed," Dr. Weiss interjected.

"Exactly so," Supreme Leader Kadahth acknowledged. "However, apparently the Katan had also picked up your temporal emanations and from that inspired a plan. Had the damage to your timeline remained, coupled with the advanced technology that Dr. Wang snuck into this device"—he held up the Chinese temporal radiation detector which Sonsa Tabbak had given to him—"and whatever else the Katan may have snuck into construction the Chinese time chamber via Dr. Wang, then it would have created a temporal cascade that would have reduced Earth to a singularity and sent time-space ripples out to neighboring star systems."

"One of which you happen to own?" Agent Hessman surmised.

"Your reasoning is once again impeccable," the Supreme Leader replied with a slight nod. "We have a base in the same sector as your planet, Earth. A key facility whose destruction would have given the Katan a significant regional advantage. All without leaving any evidence that it was the Katan behind it, since Earth would have been destroyed and with it, any telltale advanced technology, not to mention Sonsa Tabbak's vessel."

"We had no idea that's what Dr. Wang was up to," one of the Chinese suddenly burst out. "It is not our fault."

"You still had a desire to significantly alter your world's history," the Supreme Leader reminded them. "The Katan fed upon that desire, but it was still yours to begin with. Without that desire, the Katan's temptations would have fallen upon deaf ears. Your shared guilt has now been established. You will henceforth remain in silence unless told otherwise. Understood?"

Galnaran guards aimed their weapons more specifically in the direction of the Chinese group to drive the supreme leader's point home, guaranteeing their silence.

"The quick action of Sonsa Tabbak caused this plan to fail," the Supreme Leader continued, "but the programming within Dr. Wang's subconscious apparently saw an opportunity for a back-up plan."

"To assassinate yourself and this governing body," Agent Hessman surmised. "That would have no doubt thrown your government into complete chaos—at least enough for your enemy to take significant advantage of."

"Exactly so," the Supreme Leader confirmed. "Dr. Wang's altered body chemistry coupled with the insulin trigger was the perfect way of sneaking an explosive past our security system, since it was not yet an explosive at the time."

"Diabolical," Dr. Weiss remarked.

"If I understand the vernacular correctly," Supreme Leader Kadahth remarked, "I quite agree."

Meanwhile, Ben's attention was caught between what was being said and his wife by his side. "Did they tell you if it's going to be a boy or girl?" he whispered.

"Silly, it's barely a small clump of cells right now," Claire whispered back. "Nothing a regular doctor could ever pick up and certainly too early to have a sex."

"Sonsa Tabbak," the alien leader continued, "I believe prior to coming here you had assigned some people to examine the Chinese time travel chamber. What have you discovered?"

"The report came in as we were performing the deep scan of the Earthers present here," Sonsa Tabbak replied, stepping forward. "After dealing with some rather objectionable individuals trying to guard the facility, my people found that the bulk of the technology used came from the Katan. Very little of its design was of earthly origin."

"Well," Mr. Thomas whispered to Agent Hessman, "I suppose that lets your Captain Beck off the hook..."

Agent Hessman responded with a faint nod, but Mr. Thomas was not quite finished.

"... mostly."

Agent Hessman gave Mr. Thomas a questioning look but said nothing.

"As I suspected," Supreme Leader Kadahth responded to Sonsa Tabbak. "You will order your people to dismantle the Chinese time chamber immediately."

"Affirmative, Qual Ahk-Sonsa Kadahth."

Sonsa Tabbak nodded briefly, then stepped to the side as his leader continued. The Galnaran leader's gaze panned now across the entire group of Earthers, taking in every individual there. Andros took advantage of this pause to now speak up, while reaching into his jacket to pull something out.

"Esteemed leader, Qual Ahk-Sonsa Kadahth," he said, "I come with a present for you. Bottle of finest drink in all Russia." He held up the small bottle of vodka with a grin. "Only slightly used. Would like to drink toast with you but fear I had a head start."

Supreme Leader Kadahth glanced at Sonsa Tabbak with a questioning look.

"He calls it vodka," came Sonsa Tabbak's reply. "It scans as being mildly toxic but should be okay in small quantities. He drank some himself from the same bottle."

"A gift from an alien world given in sign of friendship," Supreme Leader Kadahth stated. "We never refuse symbols of friendship. We accept the gift."

Andros held the bottle high, and Supreme Leader Kadahth reached out his hand. The bottle tugged free of Andros's hand and floated up into the air, over to the supreme leader. An amphitheater full of aliens then watched as Supreme Leader Kadahth twist off the bottle top and take a small sip.

A moment later, he coughed.

Andros grinned.

"A bit like a drink common to one of our member worlds," Supreme Leader Kadahth stated.

"Then it is good?" Andros prompted.

"It feels like a kick to my throat," Supreme Leader Kadahth replied, "but it has a certain . . . quality." He then took a second small sip.

"You must be part Russian," Andros laughed. "No one in all country likes it but we all drink it, nonetheless. Then brag about it."

After the second sip, Supreme Leader Kadahth screwed the cap back on the bottle and secured it in a pocket of his robe.

"We will toast later. Right now, there is still the matter of Earth's remaining time travel capabilities."

"You're going to take it away from us, aren't you?" Dr. Weiss presumed. "All that work, all the questions that we could have answered."

"The history we could have uncovered," Ben added wistfully.

"I realize your original motives for experimenting in time travel were purely that of curiosity," the Supreme Leader stated. "That is why I am going to make you an offer. A gift. In exchange for stopping time travel from any Earth faction, we will supply a time travel monitor that will hook up to one, and only one, time chamber. Any other such chambers will be immediately dismantled."

"Do we get to choose which chamber?" Andros asked.

"It will be the American one," Supreme Leader Kadahth replied. "The Chinese faction have shown that they cannot be trusted with such capabilities."

"Just as well," Andros shrugged. "Russia time travel tech still like infant with whooping cough."

"This monitor," Supreme Leader Kadahth continued, "will allow you to see into the past like a window. It will allow you to view history directly, which I understand was your original intent. It will prohibit anyone stepping into the past in any form except under specific circumstances and with rigid limitations. It will not allow you to travel to or even view anything of the future or possible futures. Other than that, what can be so viewed will be limited by your own technology. We will install only a limiter or controller interface. As your technology improves, you may upgrade your facilities, but our time travel monitor will remain in place. Is this understood?"

Agent Hessman glanced at his historian friend, Ben, who grinned from ear to ear.

THE ALIENS STEP IN

"If I may," Ben interjected, "you mentioned that visiting the past would be allowed only under certain circumstances. What sorts of circumstances?"

"Only circumstances that you would call common sense," Supreme Leader Kadahth explained. "The parameters will be programmed into the monitor, but generally such situations such as saving something that would be lost to history anyway. A perfect example would be Mrs. Claire Hill-Stein; she was taken from the past just prior to her death, with no alteration of the timeline. Or perhaps there is some lost artifact you might wish to study that was otherwise forever lost to the depths of your oceans. Situations such as that are permissible. The device will strictly monitor such excursions and alert us to any problems. Other than that, there will be no one going back in time, and your agency will patrol itself to ensure that no more temporal events occur. Is this acceptable?"

"To still have the capability to so study the past," Ben replied, "this is a most acceptable compromise. Besides, I got what I want from the past." He pulled Claire in for a one-armed hug by his side.

"Yes," the Leader said, "and congratulations."

"We cannot speak for our government," one of the Chinese men meekly replied, though was quick to add, "but we will do our best to convince them."

"I cannot speak for my government either," Andros said, "but I feel it is something they can agree to if Americans allow Russian scientists into facility to observe."

"Well, I *can* speak for my government," Mr. Thomas stated, "and this sounds best for all. We will allow scientists from other governments into the facility to observe but only under strict protocols."

"Agreeable," Andros stated. "I will bring vodka to celebrate on first day."

"Then I'm bringing some antacids that day," Dr. Weiss said nearly under his breath.

"Besides," Mr. Thomas added, "I was close to shutting down the entire project anyway."

"I wouldn't mind studying the monitor you'll be hooking up," Dr.

Weiss remarked, "if that would be permitted."

"Of course," Supreme Leader Kadahth said. "Then if there is nothing else—"

"Just one little thing," Claire interrupted. "I make it a point to try and collect a souvenir from each time period I've gone to, or in this case, each planet. I don't suppose there is anything you might spare. Just a little knickknack."

The alien leader's features remained neutral for a moment or two. Then he reached into the pocket of his jumpsuit, pulled something out, and tossed it to Claire. It was a gem, about an inch across, glittering with rainbows and shifting images held within it like a stellar kaleidoscope, a window to infinity within her palm.

Andros's eyes widened when he saw the size of the gem.

"A simple piece of artwork," Supreme Leader Kadahth stated. "It's common enough, I sometimes use it to meditate with."

"Why, it's gorgeous," Claire exclaimed. "I've never seen anything like it!"

"And worth fortune, from looks of it," Andros remarked.

"I'll put it with my collection," Claire said, still cupping it in her hands and watching its colors dance.

"And I'll be upping the security measures around your little collection," Sue noted.

"Thank you so very much," Claire stated.

"Then if that is all, this audience is at an end," Supreme Leader Kadahth stated.

As everyone else turned away to follow Sonsa Tabbak out of the amphitheater, Agent Hessman saw Supreme Leader Kadahth reach into his robe and take another sip from the small bottle of Russian vodka.

And he saw Claire smile and glance at her camera as she recorded everything.

CHAPTER TWENTY-SIX
EXCHANGE

A FEW WEEKS LATER, AGENT HESSMAN and his team were back on Earth. The second time chamber had already been decommissioned, and alien technicians were installing new time travel monitors in the primary time chamber. General Karlson was there to supervise the whole process, while Dr. Weiss tried looking over the aliens' shoulders to see what they were doing both out of curiosity and to ensure that no one damaged his "baby" as he called it, advanced alien or not.

Sue was present with Agent Hessman to manage facility security—particularly important since one representative each from Russia and China were in attendance—and to keep eyes on the alien equipment being installed.

The Russian representative turned out to be, perhaps not so coincidentally, Andros Kortnev.

Mr. Thomas was back to being a silent background observer, for which Agent Hessman was relieved.

Sonsa Tabbak oversaw the alien side of things, standing beside General Karlson to one side of the chamber, both staying out of the way while the

THE ALIENS STEP IN

alien crew worked hand in hand with the human one.

"Sam," General Karlson called to Dr. Weiss, "how's it looking?"

"Unfathomable," came Dr. Weiss's reply as he pulled away from the travel chamber to join him.

"The operation is simple," Sonsa Tabbak explained. "Images of the time and place being viewed will form at the center of the chamber above the location where your pods would normally be located. Each image will be fully three-dimensional, just like your holograms. You merely have to walk around to study it. The monitor being installed in this chamber's control room will allow you to shift the physical location of the view from place to place within that same time period. Should such a time arise when personal transit is desired and permitted, then your pods will operate as normal, though perhaps a bit more efficiently and without as much of a chronon trail. Additionally, the rest of your technology for monitoring any time travel traffic is being upgraded. This will allow you to better track any errant temporal events in time to fix them, and it will notify us if a near catastrophic temporal event may be in progress."

"Training wheels," Dr. Weiss translated for the general's benefit.

"Got it," General Karlson replied.

The doors opened, permitting the entry of three more individuals: Claire and Ben, both beaming, with Captain Beck a step behind them.

"Look who we bumped into on the way in," Claire grinned.

"I'm out on probation," Captain Beck explained. "None of what I'd leaked to China was in itself dangerous or responsible for what happened, and since we're now on a share and share alike basis with Russia and China, the brass at the Pentagon thought it best to continue to make use of my years of experience. Or at least that's what one person convinced them of that spoke up on my behalf."

"Why General," Ben began, "how very considerate of you."

"Not me," the general replied, "though I did put in a good word."

"Then who?" Claire asked.

Captain Beck glanced over to Mr. Thomas, who was standing quietly by the wall.

"You?" Ben said with obvious surprise.

Mr. Thomas glanced back. His response was coldly efficient but lacking its usual angry snap. "Whenever possible, I do not like to waste good material or personnel. But if Captain Beck violates his probation, I still have a bullet ready for him."

That said, Mr. Thomas went back to being quiet and unobtrusive.

Agent Hessman smiled.

"That sounds like our Mr. Thomas," Ben remarked.

"I still do not like the man," Claire whispered, grimacing.

Sue strode toward Claire. "Well?" she prompted, smiling.

"The doctor finally confirmed what the alien scanner detected." Claire smiled back. "I am with child."

"That's just great," Sue replied. She gave Claire a quick hug and returned to sharply observing the personnel dashing around the chamber, human and alien alike.

"Claire," General Karlson said, "this reminds me. Those videos and pictures you took while on Galnar have had every scientist and analyst in the base very busy."

"And ones in Russia as well," Andros added.

"Glad I could contribute something," Claire replied with a smile. "And with Sonsa Tabbak's approval as well."

"It would take your best scientists at least a century to make anything out of our more critical systems from those pictures," Sonsa Tabbak remarked. "There was never any threat."

"Your article on the experience has proven popular as well," the general continued.

"In Russia also," Andros added with a grin.

"Well, that was fast," Claire giggled. "Made the rounds with all the spy agencies already."

"Part of the new exchange program, actually," General Karlson corrected. "Sonsa Tabbak, the work looks like it's progressing quite well. How soon before it will be finished?"

"It should be ready before this day is up," Sonsa Tabbak told the general. "When it is, you may engage in your first mission to test out the limiters. After that, we will leave you to observe your own history."

"Something I'm really looking forward to," Dr. Weiss said, rejoining the group. "From what I can tell, the range and efficiency of the chamber has been increased. That is indeed a gift! From what the alien techs told me, if we're back in time on a mission and someone is about to commit a temporal faux pas, those limiters Sonsa Tabbak mentioned will warn us twice. The first warning is a sharp migraine. The second warning is an abrupt yank back into the present, no questions asked."

"Understandable," General Karlson agreed. "And reasonable, given the possible dangerous alternatives."

"This shall be an opportunity for you to take a look at yourselves and your past," Sonsa Tabbak explained. "To grow as a species. Let this be a tool for your own self-examination. Then later, when you feel ready for more, we may talk again."

"Hmm, I'm not sure," Dr. Weiss mused, "but it just sounded like he said that Mankind as a race is in need of some psychotherapy."

"From what I've seen from my time to this," Claire quipped, "that is a very good possibility."

"I see," the general remarked, turning to Sonsa Tabbak. "And the alternative to therapy?"

The alien did not reply.

"They're taking away our guns and giving us water pistols, so we don't kill ourselves," Agent Hessman blandly quipped.

The remark prompted a slight grin from Sonsa Tabbak.

Meanwhile, Claire finally noticed Andros Kortnev's presence and eyed Sue. "So, how'd the latest bout go?" she asked.

"We're one and one," Sue replied. "I won the first one in Hawaii. Apparently, Russians don't do well with bare feet on hot sand."

"I know hot," Andros shot back. "That was scalding frying pan, not made for bare feet."

"One of my stipulations for the match," Sue explained. "But the next one we fought someplace a lot colder where I was numb from the knees on down."

"*Da*, and have now earned at least kiss," Andros grinned. "Though will not be having bride anytime soon."

"Such globe-trotting, it sounds like you're making a real world-tour out of this," Claire noted.

"Oh, he thinks he's sneaking in some dating time doing it this way," Sue explained with a shrug. "Tried to get me to have dinner with him after each fight."

"So, what'd you do?" Claire asked.

"I thanked him with a lukewarm handshake both times then headed straight for the airport, sighting my duties as an excuse."

"You didn't!" Claire giggled. "That was just awful."

"Pretty black woman make it difficult, but Russian not back down," Andros firmly stated. "I will win that date. This I vow."

"Only if I let him," Sue said in a quieter tone to Claire and Ben. "This *I* promise."

Claire and Ben exchanged smirks, but the Russian wasn't quite finished. "Have place in mind for third fight," he said. "Thinking wilds of primitive Manhattan."

"What wilds?" Sue said with a slight snort. "Manhattan is about as civilized as any place."

"Maybe *now*," Andros said with a suggestive glance to the time chamber where the alien techs were busy installing final hookups.

"You wouldn't," Sue gasped. "Do you know how frivolous such use of this chamber would be?"

"What's the matter?" Andros asked with a growing grin. "Pretty Black woman afraid of getting stepped on by T-Rex during contest?"

Sue replied with little more than a growl, which got Andros chuckling even more.

THE ALIENS STEP IN

Agent Hessman noticed all heads suddenly turn to the doorway behind him. And then he caught the scent. The very special scent of gardenias. He slowly turned.

No longer supported by either wheelchair or crutch, Samantha stood on her own feet, fully dressed, with no nurse in sight. In a room where aliens all around installed equipment that should have any scientist worth their salt eagerly trying to examine, Samantha had only eyes for one person. She stared forlornly in Agent Hessman's direction.

After several long seconds of standing there, Samantha stepped toward him. He couldn't speak, but he couldn't take his eyes off her.

"Lou," she said while the others returned to their own conversations.

"I'm on duty," Agent Hessman stated flatly. "No time for frivolous conversation."

"You're trying to alienate me. I realize this," Samantha said softly. "But it's not going to work. Sooner or later, you won't have your duty to hide behind, and that's when we're going to talk."

She stood there a moment longer, staring at his silence, then stepped back and turned away.

Agent Hessman's heart raced in his chest and his tongue swelled with words he longed to say but refused to speak.

Samantha dashed over to Claire. "Congratulations, Claire. You'll make a wonderful mother."

"Thank you," Claire replied.

"Yeah," Ben added, "just imagine the education this kid's going to get. The teacher mentions ancient Rome in class, and we show him what it really looked like through the time window. Math and science tutor required, and we get Dr. Weiss. Maybe for an art teacher, we can take him back for a talk with Leonardo da Vinci. Yep, all things considered, we'll have the only kid with a security clearance by the time he's four."

Agent Hessman thought Claire and Ben made relationships look too easy.

The women broke away with a light chuckle each. Samantha greeted

Ben with a warm handshake before she headed back for the door. With one last look at Agent Hessman, who maintained an overly close eye on everyone working in the chamber, she left.

Meanwhile, General Karlson was having a word with Sonsa Tabbak. "Just one thing I'm not too sure of," General Karlson said to the alien commander. "You can't simply be doing all this just to safeguard our timelines. If it were only a matter of military security, you'd just take all our toys and go. You want something else as well, but I can't figure out what it is."

"Trade, General Karlson," the alien replied.

"Trading what? What could we possibly have that you would want or need?"

"A cultural exchange," Sonsa Tabbak answered. "As my new friend, Dr. Weiss—Sam—has been telling me, my kind seems to lack what he calls the social graces. He has been educating me."

"Just things like being polite," Ben interjected. "How to greet a guest, that sort of thing. Also, when to address people by their first name only, instead of their whole, first, last, and title. Isn't that so, Tabbak?"

"Yes, Sam," Sonsa Tabbak replied. "My people also have a continuing desire to see other species' forms of art. Paintings, sculptures, even dance."

"Speaking of which," Andros said, stepping closer, "I have made arrangements for Russian Ballet to go on tour for three weeks at world of Galnar."

"Thank you, friend Andros. I also have a request from Supreme Leader Kadahtt. He was hoping that maybe you could send a case of your vodka along with the ballet company."

"It would be my pleasure!" the Russian replied with a loud chuckle. "Will also throw in some beluga caviar with instructions on how to properly consume."

"Caviar?" the alien asked.

"As with most things Russian," General Karlson warned, "it is best to enjoy first then ask afterwards."

"I see. Then I shall endeavor to urge my leader to enjoy first. But there is one other thing we would wish of you, something a little personal, if you would."

"You pulled our butts out of the temporal fires," General Karlson replied. "Name it."

For this, Sonsa Tabbak stepped over to face Claire. Her smile turned to a moment of confusion.

"Me?" she said. "What could you possibly want of me?"

"As I stated previously, we have been monitoring all temporal events occurring here on Earth, including your own trips," SonsaTabbak replied. "Trips that you have already made, trips that you still might make, and even trips that you would have made had we not intervened. For each of these, my people have found your interviews with various historical figures rather fascinating and insightful."

"How do you like that!" Claire smiled, "I'm not just popular with all the better spy agencies, but aliens as well. But then what do you want from me?"

The alien remained calm and impassive as he reached into a pocket in his jumpsuit and pulled out what looked like a pad and a simple form of writing stick. He presented them to Claire.

"Your autograph? If you wouldn't mind, of course."

Claire was not the first to grin nor the first to break out in laughter. Ben chuckled, Andros let out with a belly-laugh, and even the Chinese representative found himself in stitches.

Claire responded with a quick curtsy before taking the pad and pen. "Well, I'm flattered. I'll do it, but under one condition," she agreed. "You've got to give me a good quote. Something for my readers, of which I apparently have more than I knew."

"I will endeavor to think up something quotable, Miss—uh, Claire," Sonsa Tabbak replied with a brief glance at Dr. Weiss. The doctor nodded his approval of the more familiar form of address as Claire signed her name.

☾

Some days later, as the large alien vessel vanished from Earth-based satellite grids, a meeting was being held in one of the conference rooms. A meeting led by General Karlson, with Agent Hessman, Dr. Weiss, Sue, Ben, and Claire, Mr. Thomas observing.

"All recording devices are on," Agent Hessman said. "We may begin, General."

"Good, then first question," the general began. "What of Sonsa Tabbak's ship?"

"Leaving orbit as we speak," Dr. Weiss replied. "Or at least beyond our ability to detect. I've no doubt that they will continue to monitor our activities."

"As expected," the general said. "Lou, how went the mission? I've been so busy being in the middle of those trade deals with the Galnarans, I haven't had time to keep up. How is the time chamber doing with the new alien hookups?"

All eyes faced now to Agent Hessman, the voice for their recent excursions. "First, we used the viewing function to look back at a selection of various points in history," he said. "As Sam will confirm, the clarity of view was phenomenal, as was the temporal range. We confirmed that that Cleopatra did indeed kill herself with an asp, that William Shakespeare did indeed write everything accredited to him, and by use of slow-motion viewing, we confirmed which bullet killed Kennedy."

"Turns out it was a turkey-shoot," Sue added. "The only way they could have missed him is if he'd never shown up at all."

"With Sonsa Tabbak watching," Agent Hessman continued, "we then tested out their limiter system by trying various ways to try and get the chamber to connect to a future time. Nothing worked."

"That's a relief," General Karlson replied. "That future stuff was problematic enough as it was."

"I can tell the president he has one less thing to worry about," Mr. Thomas interjected. "What about actual physical translation through time?"

THE ALIENS STEP IN

"Well, again with Sonsa Tabbak in observance, we picked a time and place guaranteed to produce absolutely no temporal disruptions," Agent Hessman stated. "Even with the increased sensitivity of the new equipment and Claire asking all her reporter questions."

"There was a lot of stuff the movies got wrong," Claire added, "even after allowing for dramatic license. Got a number of great interviews with dead people. Well, people who are dead *now*."

"It got a bit scary once the ship started to sink," Ben picked up. "We would have left a little sooner than we did, but my wife was intent on getting some good perspectives and quotes."

"I'm not going to let one little iceberg stop me," Claire grinned.

"Our unsinkable Claire Hill-Stein," Dr. Weiss chuckled.

"Also, I came back with a souvenir," Claire added. "A sextant from the captain's quarters. Nothing that ever appeared on the list of what they got when they dredged up the wreck."

"So, if I'm hearing this correctly, you visited the Titanic on her maiden voyage," General Karlson summarized. "And no temporal anomalies?"

"Not a one," Sue reported. "Though we did try to create some just to test the system."

"It was one of those events where nothing we could have done would have ever changed it," Dr. Weiss added. "We had a list of known survivors, so we knew who to avoid. And then I tried to introduce myself as a time traveler to one man on the survivor's list."

"And what happened?" Mr. Thomas asked.

"Before I could even get a word out, I got a rather intense headache as warning. Yet when Claire introduced herself as a time-traveling reporter to another person we knew was not to survive, nothing happened. Everything worked just as it was supposed to. Sonsa Tabbak confirmed everything before he returned to his vessel."

"And Captain Beck?" the general asked.

"On his best behavior," Agent Hessman stated. "In fact, he kept the captain of the ship busy long enough once for Claire to do some prowling around the bridge area."

"Excellent," General Karlson decided. "Then I'm going to open up the chamber for wider use, though keeping it mostly to viewing only. Both the Russians and Chinese have stated their interest in seeing certain portions of their own history. I will allow that but only when our people are present. Sam, a lot of times that's going to be you, probably with Sue around as well. And Ben as our resident historian."

"Samantha is more than well enough now to also act as a monitor," Dr. Weiss suggested. "She's been itching for something to do."

"I will take that under advisement with our security chief... Lou." He looked over to Agent Hessman.

Agent Hessman gave a noncommittal nod.

"I've had a system programmed where scientists from any country whose government is in on our little secret can submit a request for temporal viewing," General Karlson continued. "Mainly so everyone doesn't crowd in at once. Agent Hessman's team will vet every single viewing candidate. Similarly, any request for actual in-person visits to some period back in history will likewise be vetted, but requirements for those approvals will be extremely strict, with final approval required from a unanimous vote of myself, Mr. Thomas, Lou, Sam, and Ben. Essentially, this will comprise our temporal board of supervisors. Any objections?"

"I'm not on the board?" Sue asked.

From the expression on her face, she was only half serious with that question, but the general gave it a very serious answer.

"You are part of Lou's team, but you also have a very specific function that Mr. Thomas here insisted upon."

"And what might that be?" Claire asked.

Mr. Thomas proceeded to explain. "Any time an in-person trip back into time is approved, especially if it includes nationals from another country, you are to monitor the travelers. If you ever see someone get one of those headache warnings and fail to heed it, or if you catch them otherwise plotting to do something that might undermine the timeline while trying

THE ALIENS STEP IN

to get around the safety protocols the aliens established, you have the authority to terminate their trip—even if it's with a bullet to their brain. This authority comes direct from the president, as well the leaders of Russia, China, and Great Britain. Am I absolutely clear?"

"I'm double-oh Sue, licensed to kill," Sue grinned.

"Exactly," Mr. Thomas said with his usual lack of humor.

"And what about Captain Beck?" Agent Hessman asked. "He can be an asset for the rare in-person trips back and has been comporting himself within regulations."

"He only goes if his skillset is required for a given mission," General Karlson decided, "and only with Sue along on the same mission. You understand what that means, Agent Harris."

"Yes, sir," Sue replied. "If he steps out of line, it will be my duty to handle him just like any other. But he'll behave."

"He'd better do so," General Karlson stated. "That should about cover things then. Good job with the system test."

"Oh, one small thing, General," Sue said. "If you could allow me a couple days off next week, I would appreciate it."

"Might this have something to do with that third fight with the Russian?" The general's tone was serious, his gaze level, but Sue would not be cowed and met it with an even gaze.

"To be blunt, yes."

"Well then, I suppose I'll have to say yes. But under one condition." His serious expression broke quite gradually into a slowly rising grin before he continued. "I've got ten dollars in the pool on you winning, so he'd better not earn any more than that one win."

"Of course not, sir. And . . . there's a betting pool going on about this?"

"Half the base," Ben told her. "If he wins, he gets half the money to use on the date. If you win, you get half the money to do whatever you feel like doing to embarrass him. Even Mr. Thomas is in for five."

"On behalf of the president," Mr. Thomas answered quickly. "It's a matter of national pride."

"Then as a matter of national pride," Sue grinned, "I'd best make him lick my boots."

"You do that," the general told her. "Meeting adjourned."

Everyone stood and began filing out, with Agent Hessman at the rear.

CHAPTER TWENTY-SEVEN
AGENT HESSMAN'S DECISION

AGENT LOU HESSMAN WAS THE last one out the door from the conference room, but that was on purpose, for he knew who would be waiting for him on the other side. Just as he had suspected, Samantha was standing there, ready to intercept him with an arm across the door frame. She waited until the others had walked far enough down the hall and gone onto wherever it was each was headed before speaking.

"You have been avoiding me for three weeks now," she began. "You can't simply dump me and move on. We need to talk."

"Samantha, I—"

"No."

She moved her arm from the doorway and placed a hand to his chest, lightly shoving him back into the conference room and closing the door behind her.

"I realize your reasoning for wanting to distance yourself from any relationships. Your job is dangerous. I get that," Samantha said. "You're afraid of endangering anyone connected with you. I get that too. But I read the report of what happened on Galnar. About how that Chinese woman had been programmed just like me, only she didn't come out of it. The report blames the advanced alien tech used on her, of course, but I know better. Alien tech, future tech, it makes no difference. In each case, we were a bunch of monkeys compared to that stuff."

Samantha poked Agent Hessman in the chest. "You know what *really* made the difference? You, Lou. You saved me just the way you saved a lot of other people. You saved me because we meant something to each other. Dr. Wang was doomed because her heart didn't have anyone there to protect it."

Samantha stepped back a bit to look Lou in the eye, while he continued to remain silent and stare at his shoes.

"I came through it because I knew there was someone out here pulling for me," Samantha continued. "I can take care of myself, and I have every confidence that should things get rough, you'll be there for me just as you would any other team member. But distancing yourself from . . . from us, denying what your heart wants? That longing in itself will interfere with your work just as much as having me on the team. Maybe even more. There has to be some middle ground."

She paused for a moment, her eyes welling up with tears that she did not try to hold back. For a long moment she simply looked him in the eyes and let her tears do her speaking.

"Lou," she finally said, "I love you. And I don't care if it's Russians from the future, aliens from whatever planets are out there, or creatures from beneath the ocean. I'm not about to let anyone else make the decision about how we should live. You've been afraid to say it, but despite that professionally bland expression, I can see it in your eyes; you love me too. All you have to do is admit it to yourself."

Samantha paused once more, only a moment this time, before drawing in a breath to speak again. But before she could continue arguing her case, Agent Hessman raised his right hand and pressed his forefinger lightly to her lips. He gazed into her eyes and studied the mix of emotions fountaining from her eyes and down her cheeks.

Then, for the first time in weeks, he finally spoke to her. Just two words. "Let's talk..."

ILLUSTRATIONS

1	Chinese Temporal Data Recorder	55
2	Sonsa Tabback - Alien Captain	79
3	Galnaran Space Ship	87
4	Dicta-Ring	93
5	Galnaran Ship Manufacturing Bay	95
6	Galnaran Ship Power Generator	97
7	The Bridge	99
8	Western Ghost Town	101
9	Galnaran Shuttle Craft	125
10	Wormhole	131
11	Galnar from Space	134
12	Hall of Governance	136
13	City of Serta	138
14	Tasha Ray'ahl - Galnaran Escort	143
15	Amphitheater	170
16	Qual Ahk-Sonsa Kadahth Supreme Leader	177
17	Galnaran Time Chamber	199

CPSIA information can be obtained
at www.ICGtesting.com
Printed in the USA
BVHW012039210623
666217BV00010B/137